THE

THE TOY BREAKER

PAUL ROGERS

illustrated by
Emma Rogers

RED FOX

A Red Fox Book

Published by Random House Children's Books
20 Vauxhall Bridge Road, London SW1V 2SA

A division of The Random House Group Ltd
London Melbourne Sydney Auckland
Johannesburg and agencies throughout the world

1 3 5 7 9 10 8 6 4 2

First published in Great Britain by
The Bodley Head Children's Books,
1999

Red Fox edition 2000

Printed and bound in Great Britain by Cox & Wyman Ltd,
Reading, Berkshire

THE RANDOM HOUSE GROUP Limited Reg. No. 954009

www.randomhouse.co.uk

ISBN 0 09 940433 8

Contents

For Emma

1
The Trouble Begins

Jamie and Liddy were in the same class at school. Apart from that, not much else about them was the same. Jamie lived with his mum in a tiny house that would have fitted comfortably into Liddy's dining room. If he wanted something, he and his mum had to save up for it. Whereas Liddy had everything she wanted. But that was not the trouble. The trouble was that she had everything Jamie wanted too.

It was a Saturday. Jamie had been invited to her house to play, for the first time. He was doing his best not to look envious, but he was feeling it all right. Liddy knew he was feeling it and that was exactly why she'd invited him. She had already shown him (or rather shown off to him)

her cat
her videos
her computer
her playstation
her music centre
her puppet theatre
her stamp collection.

Now she was showing him her collection of holiday souvenirs. 'I got this when we went skiing,' she said, holding up one of those glass scenes that snow when you turn them upside down. She handed it to Jamie.

Just then her mum called: 'Lydia darling! Time for milkshake!'

'Coming, Mummy,' Liddy chirped and she ran out of the room ahead of Jamie.

They spent the rest of the afternoon playing downstairs until Jamie's mum came to collect Jamie. Liddy's mother, Mrs Grabham-Popham, a lady with a very large bust who wore enough gold jewellery to fill a shop window, closed the front door on them with a sigh of relief. It wasn't that the boy was badly behaved, and he looked clean enough. It was just that he wasn't really the type of child Lydia ought to be making friends with.

Mrs Grabham-Popham was just wondering

how to explain this to her daughter, when Liddy let out a gut-wrenching scream from upstairs in her bedroom.

'Oh, sweetie, what is it?' cried her mother, launching herself up the carpeted curve of the staircase. But Liddy couldn't give her much of an answer. Instead of words, it was mainly gasps and shrieks that came out of her. 'It's! . . . him! . . . he's! . . . that! . . . he's! . . . my! . . .'

The sight that met her mother's eyes as she burst into the room told it all. On the floor lay Liddy's precious Canadian snowstorm

broken
shattered
scattered
in sharp
ruined
jagged
destroyed
splinters
wrecked
smashed
dashed
into a hundred
smithereens
to pieces

'It was that boy!' Liddy wailed. 'He did it on purpose! I know he did!'

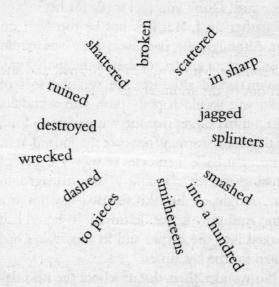

'How do you know?' said her mother. 'It might have been the cat.'

'It was him! He had it in his hands when you called us for tea! And anyway, the cat's been asleep all day!'

Mrs Grabham-Popham took her daughter in her arms and pressed her to her bosom.

'I'm never asking him here again!' sobbed Liddy.

Over her head, her mother's face broke into a contented smile.

Poor girl! Don't you feel sorry for her?

Neither do I. But let's not be too hard on her. Although she had everything you could possibly want (and a number of things that you couldn't), and although she was the sort of child you would happily push into a puddle, you mustn't forget that she was genuinely fond of that snowstorm. Whenever she looked at it, it brought back memories of snowy slopes, of adoring parents clapping as she managed to stay upright on her skis for two seconds at a time. And now it was destroyed. Its liquid had soaked into the carpet and its snowflakes had fallen for the last time.

No wonder, then, that at school the next day it was the first thing she wanted to tell everyone. 'Do you know what?' she hissed to one huddled group after another. 'That horrible Jamie smashed one of my favourite toys!'

'Really?' they'd say, and 'You're joking!' And they'd stare poisonously across the playground at the unfortunate Jamie, who to begin with had no idea what it was all about. Of course, everyone was very sympathetic, because everyone wanted to be Liddy's friend, because everyone wanted to be invited to play at Liddy's house, because everyone knew that Liddy had so many things to play with, because Liddy had told them.

Now as you know, any awful piece of news is exciting as long as it doesn't affect you personally. (That's why grown-ups love watching the news on television, though they pretend it's because they need to know what's going on.) So this shocking piece of news about Liddy's snowstorm ran round the playground like chickenpox. As for those children who hadn't been to her house yet and thought that they should have been invited rather than Jamie, they were especially pleased that her choice had proved so unwise, and they did their best to shake up every flake of hatred in Liddy.

But no one was more shocked than Jamie when he heard it. And this was for one very simple reason: because it wasn't true. Jamie had not broken Liddy's snowstorm. He had put it carefully back on the shelf in front of the African mask and the boomerang. Which is what he told Liddy when she eventually came up, surrounded by a gang of ill-wishers, to tell him how much she hated him.

Did anyone believe Jamie? Of course they didn't! Jamie had holes in his jumper and worn out trainers that were not a famous make in the first place. It was exactly the sort of thing that someone like that would do - someone poor envious of someone rich - wasn't it?

By the end of playtime, the playground looked like this:

Samantha Michael Lizzy Christine
Natasha Sandra Matthew A. Liddy
Simon Emma Jeremy
Louise Ludovic Andrea
Terry Helen Jonathan
Solomon Winston
Becky Brett
Matthew M. Ben
Thomas **Jamie** William
Katy Giles Roxanne
Tom Cathy
Marcus Robby
Vikki Lionel Martin Ndeye Wayne
Jason Alice
Bobby Anne-Marie Myriam

Jamie was so relieved when the school bell rang to call them back to lessons.

It was a real bell, perched in a little turret on the roof, and could be heard from a long way off. At the sound of it, parents in houses all around the district thought of their little offspring, some with a warm glow, others with a feeling of deep thankfulness that someone else was looking after them. Miss Clement, Jamie's teacher, gave one last tug on the bellrope and waited for her class to come in.

Miss Clement always wore unbelievably long cardigans - as if she tied bricks to them when they were hanging on the washing line. She was kind, in a bossy sort of way. But right now she seemed ruffled.

'Children,' she said solemnly, 'something very bad has happened, something I wouldn't have expected of Class Seven. I don't know who it was, but somebody has damaged the lovely ship that Tom brought in to show us.'

Twenty-nine heads turned to the table by the window. There was a chorus of twenty-eight gasps and one wail.

Its beautiful mast was snapped.

'Ship' wasn't a grand enough word for it: it was a galleon. But now its figurehead was broken and across the gold and red planking of its hull, running right from bows to stern, was a hideous, deliberate scratch!

Tears were pouring down Tom's cheeks like rain down a windowpane.

'Now,' said Miss Clement, 'do any of you know anything about it?'

A wave of whispers washed round the room.

There was a silence. Then, 'Jamie was the last out!' someone piped up.

It was true. He'd had to wait to borrow someone's felt-tips because his own had dried up. He'd stayed behind to finish his map.

'Yes,' called someone else, 'Jamie must have done it!'

Have you ever watched a pack of lions closing in for the kill? Once the first fangs have brought their victim down, the others - even those who've been keeping their distance - can't wait to rush in and tear the carcass apart. Jamie didn't have much meat on him, but everyone wanted their bite.

2
Do It Yourself

As Jamie walked home from school that day, he felt more fed up than he'd felt for ages. Why had they all turned on him like that? And how was he going to get out of it? He couldn't prove that he hadn't done it.

He opened the front door, remembering not to use the handle (it usually came off in his hand), stepped over the hole where the floorboards had been up for weeks, ducked under a dangling light switch, and squeezed past the pile of bricks into the kitchen.

'I'm home,' he called, lifting the biscuit tin out of a cupboard whose doors were still waiting to be put on.

That afternoon he found his mum plastering the ceiling in his bedroom. Anyone who's ever tried plastering anything will know that it's much more difficult than it looks. But plastering a ceiling, unless you're an expert, is near enough impossible. And Jamie's mum was not an expert. Why was she doing it then? Well, for a start, she couldn't have afforded to pay anyone else to do it, even if she'd wanted to. But it wasn't just that: Jamie's mum was one of that strange breed they call D.I.Y. enthusiasts.

D.I.Y.– I expect you know – stands for 'Do It Yourself'. It's a funny name, if you think about it, to give to all that fitting and building and decorating that some people actually do for fun. After all, the words 'Do it yourself' are usually said in a fairly impatient tone of voice. Think of the times when people say it:

- When you want your bottom wiped (four years old)
- When you want your shoelace tied (eight years old)
- When you want to copy someone's homework (twelve years old)
- When you want someone to wash your socks for you (forty-seven years old)

Still, that's what it's called: Do It Yourself, and Jamie's mum did it.

So why was she plastering the ceiling in the first place? She was plastering the ceiling because she had just repaired a big hole in it. And there was a big hole in it because several weeks ago she had come bursting through it. She'd been clambering about in the attic, up to another bit of D.I.Y. Jamie had been lying on his bed at the time, practising his signature, when WHAM! - with a shriek and a huge explosion of dust and rubble, his mother's legs had suddenly appeared above his head, poking out of the ceiling. Fortunately, her thighs got wedged in the hole and stopped her coming any further. Otherwise she might have landed right on top of him.

'Well?' she said now, as Jamie came into the room. She smiled down at him from the stepladder, her face a galaxy of white speckles, 'What do you think? That's a bit better, isn't it?'

Jamie looked around. The ceiling, it was true, looked a bit better. But everything else looked a bit worse. There was plaster on the half-papered walls, on the bare lightbulb, on the legless bed propped up on bricks, on the cassette player with its speakers hanging out, on the curtains waiting to be hung, on the mirror that had come off the wall,

The ladder itself had escaped pretty lightly.

A few dollops of plaster clung to its rungs.

But this was nothing to the array of splats and blobs that had landed everywhere else.

on the wonky bookshelf

on the window he couldn't open because his mum had shut it before the paint was dry

on the football poster that covered a stain

on the door that wouldn't shut without jamming

on the lamp shade sitting on the floor

on the carpet which was too big and curled up at the walls

The biggest splodge of all sat like a meringue on Jamie's mum's head, anchored in her hair.

There was only one place where virtually no plaster had landed, an that was the square of dustcloth that his mum had stretched over Jamie's desk.

She blinked down at him from the ladder.

'Something wrong?' she asked.

Should he tell her what had happened at school? What would she be able to do about it? It would only make her feel sad.

'No,' he said, and gave a little twitch of a smile to prove it. Then he burrowed his hands into his pockets and wandered out of the room.

That evening, as they sat facing each other over their macaroni cheese, Jamie's mum was still sure that something was wrong.

'Is it your room?' she said. 'I'll do some more work on it soon.'

But Jamie said it was just that he wasn't feeling too good, and he went to bed early. He lay on his back, gazing up at the uneven white patch on the ceiling and hoping the plaster wouldn't drop out, and wondering whether to stay away from school and pretend he was ill. By the time he fell asleep, he was certain that that was what he was going to do. But in the morning it seemed like too bare-faced a lie. Jamie put on his trainers and set off for school as usual.

In class, some of the girls darted mean looks at him. He tried ignoring them. He tried sticking his tongue out at them. But whatever he tried only seemed to force him further into his shell. When they had to copy a flag, no one would lend him their colours. When they did P.E., no one wanted to be his partner.

At lunchtime, he sidled up to Samantha and Matthew. They at least used to be his friends.

'You don't believe I did it, do you?' he asked them.

They looked shiftily at each other, as if they weren't sure what to say.

Suddenly, Jamie's patience snapped. 'Thanks a lot!' he shouted. 'Great friends you are! A pity it wasn't your things that got broken!'

In view of what happened next, this was certainly not the best thing to have said.

3
Missing

Matthew MacFaddle had been given a magnificent jigsaw for his birthday. It was a picture of the animals boarding Noah's ark. They were all behaving terribly well, lining up as meekly as sheep. Even the lions were controlling their murderous instincts and waiting patiently behind a couple of wombats on the gangplank. They could obviously tell that it was a chance in a million to have been picked for the trip. And when you saw God's ocean rising ominously in the background, you could see why.

Jigsaws occupied a special place in the MacFaddle's household. They were Mrs MacFaddle's hobby. She spent all her spare time doing them – mind-stewing monstrosities of five, eight, ten thousand pieces. And she didn't go for the ones that were crammed with tell-tale details either. No, the puzzles she chose were of huge cloudy skies or fields full of poppies - thousands of tiny pieces that all looked the same. Some days she only managed to add one or two pieces to the picture. But she didn't mind. She enjoyed it! And each time she finished one, her husband glued it to a board, framed it and hung it on the wall.

So you see, jigsaws were a kind of religion in Matthew's house. This Noah's ark was the most beautiful, most difficult puzzle he had ever attempted and it was destined to join the gallery of his mother's when it was finished. He had been working on it for over two weeks. It had five hundred pieces and now there were only five left on the table. He fitted the first of them, the second, the third. Then a horrible, sick feeling flooded his mind as he stared at the hole in the middle. Something was missing!

'Muuuum!' he screamed. Mrs MacFaddle came running. One glance from her expert eye was enough to grasp the enormity of the disaster. It was the jigsaw lover's nightmare!

'Help me look on the floor!' she squawked.

Together, they fell to their knees and began crawling under the table.

'Do you remember dropping one?' she asked frantically.

'No,' replied Matthew, his chin quivering.

'Have you checked in the box?'

'Yes.'

'Do you remember seeing it?'

'Yes. No. I don't know.'

For the rest of the day they combed the room, then the house, looking for that jigsaw piece that showed a zebra's head and a baboon's bottom. But it was nowhere to be found.

Yet this was nothing compared to what was going on only a few streets away, in Samantha Gorp's house. For here too a massive search was underway, and Mr and Mrs and all three little Gorps were engaged upon it.

Samantha had a favourite bear, called Albert. He had brown, glass eyes and a wonky smile. She'd had him since she was a baby. He had become a bit bow-legged and his fur was worn, but Samantha loved him all the more for that. What a cruel, hideous shock then, when she got home from school, to find that one of his eyes was missing – plucked out of his face! She burst into tears and a moment later into her brother and sister's room, clutching the helpless victim.

'Which of you did this?' she shouted.

Their mouths fell open. It was obvious they'd had nothing to do with it.

'Someone must have done it! It couldn't just fall off! It's been yanked out on purpose!'

At this point her parents intervened.

Mr Gorp was a very slow, methodical man. His face was slack and baggy, as if it were a couple of sizes too big for his head. 'When was the last time you saw him?' he asked solemnly.

'This morning, in bed,' sniffed Samantha.

'And he had it then, did he?'

Samantha nodded. Albert stared pitifully at her from his one remaining eye. That wonky smile made him look as if he was trying to be brave.

Her dad was doing a mental calculation.

'So it must have disappeared some time between this morning and now,' he explained.

Mrs Gorp, who was always guided by her husband's wisdom, waited on his advice.

'Well,' he concluded, 'it's got to be somewhere.' This seemed to reassure him, though it didn't do much for Samantha.

And so the hunt began. They started in Samantha's room. Centimetre by centimetre, they worked their way across the carpet, advancing on all fours with their noses to the floor and their bottoms in the air. Then they shook out the bedclothes, layer by layer. Then they emptied Samantha's cupboards, then her drawers, one thing at a time.

Nothing.

'If it's not here,' declared Mr Gorp, as if he'd made a major breakthrough in human knowledge, 'it must be somewhere else.'

But two hours and every room later, they still hadn't found it. Now even Mr Gorp was looking worried.

Have you ever lost anything precious? If so, perhaps you've known that mounting panic as you scour again places you've already searched – as you find yourself looking in places where it couldn't possibly be. Mrs Gorp poured the contents of the sugar bowl through a sieve. She emptied the cornflakes packet. She turned inside out every pocket in every wardrobe in the house. Meanwhile Mr Gorp heaved cupboards away from walls and poked behind radiators.

Nothing.

After that he took up the stair carpet, groped down the sides of the sofa,

cleaned out the yucky U-tube under the sink with his bare hands, and prised up several floorboards under the stairs in case the eye had gone down one of the cracks. By the end of the evening he had found, and collected in a little heap . . .

a pen top
bits of Lego
a paperclip a tooth
a crumpled envelope
various pebbles a toffee
a thimble
a postcard buttons a pencil
a spat-out sweet
a tyre from a toy car a hanky
a comb four drawing pins
a dead spider
some beads pine needles
half a biscuit
some withered holly berries
a rubber band
a battery some silver paper
an earring
two keys
a lump of modelling clay a bookmark
a used plaster
a metal spring
a postage stamp some hardened chewing gum
a hairslide
a badge
two marbles a doll's hat
a shrivelled conker an empty cotton reel a piece of chalk
an apple core a safety pin
a burst balloon
six coins a dead match a bus ticket two screws
a champagne cork a shoelace a baby's sock
a pink ribbon a teaspoon two playing cards
a dried flower
a curtain hook three seashells
a twenty gram weight
a bent straw a clothes peg
a birthday cake candle
three magnetic letters
a green feather a domino a plastic camel and a mummified mouse

but no eye.

Poor Samantha was desperate. Then her dad, with a cobweb draped across his head, suddenly had a brainwave.

'The vacuum cleaner!' he cried. 'It's probably been hoovered up!'

Moments later he was on his knees groping through the squalid, grey contents of the hoover bag, pulling apart the matted mass of hair and fluff, while a cloud of dust gently settled all over him. Samantha's heart sank as he finished sifting through the filth - in vain.

He took hold of the vacuum cleaner to hoover up the mess and, trying to think where else they might look, asked his wife to plug it in. But poor man! He had forgotten to put back the bag and close the lid. As the machine came on, it belched out a huge smut of muck -

whoooOOOsh!

- right into his face!

'Aaaah! Urrrgh!' he spluttered, staggering backwards into the table.

Even Samantha couldn't help grinning.

'I don't understand it,' he said, as his wife helped pick the tufts of fluff and fur out of his nostrils, 'I just don't understand it.'

'You forgot to shut it,' she told him.

'No no,' he said, 'not that. Teddy's eye, I mean. We've looked everywhere. It can't have just disappeared. There's got to be an explanation.'

Of course, he was right. There was an explanation. But as you'll see, it was so unexpected, so strange, that anyone as slow-witted as Mr Gorp would find it very difficult to believe.

4
A Chance Meeting

People don't like to say so, but sometimes what's bad news for one person can be rather good news for another.

Jamie hoped that the horrible things that had happened to Matthew and Samantha would be good for him. Nobody in their right mind could claim that he had had anything to do with them. And when the others heard about them at school, one or two did begin to think that perhaps Jamie hadn't broken that model galleon after all.

'Maybe he didn't smash that thing of yours either,' Wayne suggested to Liddy.

'Of course he did!' snapped Liddy. 'Who else could have done it? No one else was there!'

A boy called Jonathan said, 'I saw this programme on telly that I'm not supposed to watch, about some aliens from another galaxy who invaded this town and made people start killing each other.'

'This town?!' gasped Wayne, his eyes nearly popping out.

'Not this town, no. This town on telly.'

'Do you think people'll start killing each other here?' asked Alice excitedly.

'No, stupid,' said Jonathan. 'But I mean, maybe it's aliens who are making all these things happen.'

'You might have aliens in your house, but I haven't got aliens in mine!' said Liddy proudly. 'We've got burglar alarms and smoke alarms in every room.'

'Yeah, but you haven't got alien alarms!' Wayne told her.

'I expect we'll be getting them soon,' said Liddy.

Then Jonathan had another idea.

'What if Jamie did it by remote control? I've heard of people who can do things like that. They can snap a fork just by staring at it. They can break a glass just by thinking about it!'

'But why should he?' said Wayne.

'Because he's jealous, of course,' said Liddy, who liked this idea. 'He hasn't got all the things that some of us have. Why else do you think he broke my snowstorm?'

Samantha felt a shiver go down her spine.

'Do you remember what he said to us yesterday?' she asked Matthew. 'He said it was a pity it wasn't *our* things that had been spoiled.'

'Well there you are,' said Jonathan. 'He probably went home and wished like mad that something of yours would get broken.'

'Well I think you're all being horrible,' said Wayne suddenly. 'I bet you wouldn't like it if *you* didn't have any money!'

'Oh come on!' said Liddy. 'It's their own fault if they're poor.'

'No it's not,' said Wayne.

'Whose fault is it then?' asked Liddy. But Wayne had no answer for that. The others started chanting:

'Wayne, Wayne, go away!
Come again another day!'

So Wayne went off and told Jamie – as if he didn't feel bad enough already – what the others had been saying about him.

All that afternoon Jamie sat in a cloud of gloom. Was it true that he was bubbling with envy? He did wish he had things some of the other children had. It didn't seem fair that he couldn't afford them. Was that envy? Was that wrong? His mum had often said to him it wasn't what you had that mattered. But he knew there were things she would have liked to have – like a car, or nice clothes – that other people didn't think twice about having.

Suddenly Miss Clement was looming over him asking why he hadn't done any work. He could feel everyone looking his way but he couldn't be bothered to make up an excuse. He put his head down and counted the minutes till the bell.

When he got home, his mum was out doing her cleaning job. She'd left some money and a note for him on the kitchen table, asking him to go and buy some fish and chips. And it was just as well she had. Because if he hadn't been sent out for fish and chips, he might never have come across Mr Isaiah Patchett. And if he hadn't come across Mr Patchett – well, you'll soon see . . .

This is how it happened. When Jamie got to their usual chippie, he found a sign in the window saying 'Closed for refurbishment'. He had no idea what 'refurbishment' meant, but 'closed' was clear enough. He knew there was another fish and chip shop not too far away, though he wasn't entirely sure how to get to it. Still, he guessed that if he cut through the old town centre he should end up somewhere near it.

Smolton wasn't a big town, so there wasn't much danger of getting lost. But the middle of it was a maze of very old, narrow streets that you could wander in for ages and still find places that you'd never seen before. Jamie entered it by a little road whose high buildings seemed to lean in towards each other. You could see it had been built for carts and not for cars. Pulleys, that had once been used to haul sacks up into the pointed lofts, stuck out into the narrow strip of sky above his head. There was a thin pavement on each side of the street – so thin that one dustbin was enough to block it. A cold wind was blowing now. It chased a bit of litter but couldn't catch it. With his collar turned up and his hands in his pockets, Jamie strolled along, enjoying the feeling that he wasn't in any particular hurry.

Every building was different from the next, with doors and windows all of different colours, shapes and sizes. There were gateways and arches, passages, porches and intriguing hatches in the pavement. One was open and

Jamie could see a chute that dived down into the secrecy of a cellar. On he walked, turning a corner here, taking a short cut through an alleyway there. He walked past offices and flats, warehouses and shops, studios and storerooms. From high-up windows came the sounds of music, of mealtimes, of machines. But there was no one about. A lone dog cocked its leg against a drainpipe. Then suddenly Jamie came into a street he had never noticed before and there in front of him was a window full of models and dolls and toys, but crowded and dusty, as if they had been put there years ago and forgotten about. What was it? He looked up and saw a sign:

Jamie burned with curiosity to see what was inside. A bell clattered as he pushed open the heavy, dark door.

'In the back!' someone called.

Jamie looked around him, amazed, at the toymender's workshop. They had had workshops at school – a drama workshop and a pottery workshop – but 'workshop' had always seemed to him a stupid name for it: they didn't work and it wasn't a shop. But this was a real workshop! A honeycomb of shelves and cubicles lined the walls, and in the middle were workbenches cluttered with tools and materials, pots and paintbrushes.

'In the back!' the voice repeated. Jamie ducked past a curtain and found himself in an even more cluttered den. No daylight entered it at all. Over a wooden bench stooped a grey-haired man holding a hammer. He wore a coat so covered in stains and smears that you could only just tell it had once been white.

'Is there something you want mending?' the man asked, carrying on with his work.

'No,' said Jamie.

'You've come to collect something?'

'No.'

'Well what do you want then?'

Jamie felt awkward. He didn't know what he wanted.

'Don't tell me you just came in for a fit of bun,' said the man.

'A what?' said Jamie.

'A bit of fun.'

'I was just interested,' said Jamie. 'Do you mind?'

The toymender put down his hammer and straightened his back slowly and painfully. He took a proper look at Jamie for the first time. And Jamie took a proper look at him.

If you were hoping for a jolly, rosy cheeked, Santa Claus type with a welcoming chuckle and a twinkle in his eye, you're going to be disappointed. This toymender had a long, thin nose and tired-looking eyes. There was no colour in his cheeks. It didn't look as if a real smile had crossed his face for years.

'Isaiah Patchett, Toymender,' he said. 'Used to be Toymaker, in the days before all this electronic nonsense; in the days when toys were toys and left you something to imagine when you played with them. But things changed. So I got rid of the ache and settled for an end.'

'The ache?' said Jamie. 'Backache, do you mean?'

'Ha!' went the toymender. 'That'll be the day, when I get rid of that! No. The "ache" in toymaker. I painted it out and wrote "end" instead: I became a toymender. But people don't believe in mending any more. Why get Patchett to patch it when you can bet a grand new one?'

Does he mean 'get a brand new one'? Jamie thought.

'Perhaps people don't know you're here,' Jamie suggested. 'I didn't know you were here.'

'Huh! I sometimes wonder if I'm here myself.'

Jamie couldn't help feeling sorry for him, even if he did seem a bit grumpy. Suddenly he had an idea.

'Do you mend teddy bears' eyes?' he asked.

'Eyes, ears, pegs, laws, anything.'

He must mean legs and paws, thought Jamie.

'What about a broken boat?' he asked.

'Have to see it.'

'And those things - you know - that snow when you turn them upside down. Can you mend them?'

'Why? Have you broken all those?'

'No,' said Jamie quickly. 'I haven't broken anything.'

'Well why ask then?' said the toymender impatiently, going back to his work.

'The thing is, I know lots of people whose toys have been broken,' said Jamie. 'But it's not them who did it. They don't know who did it.' He didn't dare say that people thought he was to blame.

Suddenly the toymender stopped working and put down his tools.

'A bear's eye, you said?'

'Yes. My friend Samantha's. Why?'

'Has she got the eye?'

'No. That's the trouble. She couldn't find it.'

For a minute Jamie felt really uncomfortable

under the toymender's gaze, as if he were being suspected again himself.

'Tell me about the other things,' said the toymender.

I don't need to tell you what Jamie said, because you already know what had happened. But the toymender's face grew more and more worried as the story went on, and he ended up looking positively alarmed.

'Oh dear,' he said at last.

'What's wrong?' Jamie asked.

'Well,' began the toymender, 'I can't be certain, but . . .'

'But what?' said Jamie.

'I may have rot it all gong,' he said, 'but this sounds to me like the work of the Toybreaker. I'd better tell you about him, because if it is, we're in for a bad time, a very bad time.'

5
The Toymender's Tale

Imagine a really horrible creature, a real little devil.

No good. That's not nasty enough.

Think of someone you really don't like. What's the nastiest thing about them? Now imagine someone who's all like that - all nastiness - with no nicer side to them at all. Too difficult?

All right. Try this. Think of a time when you've wanted to do something really mean to somebody else - something really, really mean. Don't tell me you've never felt that! Of course we all pretend we haven't, but everybody has. So: this really nasty thing that you wanted to do - or perhaps you actually did it? - imagine feeling that all the time, about everybody. Now we're getting a bit closer.

The Toybreaker was a mean-minded, spiteful little creature who took a delight in making children unhappy. He had a skinny body and moved in a twitching, jerky sort of way. A spiky stump of tail stuck out behind through a hole in the filthy, ragged clothes he wore. His head was small and pointed, with only a few tufts of orange hair on it, and his eyes, which never blinked, stared out from deep wells in a face as mean as a weasel's. The expression on it was so sneaky, so sly, that it made you want to slap him. But though he looked slappable enough, he knew how to make himself so thin that he could slide under a door, and so slippery that no hand could ever catch him.

Breaking toys was his only pleasure in life. With all his fiendish experience, he knew exactly how to achieve the greatest effect with the least effort. A quick snap here, a yank there, a poke, a twist, a rip. One stolen jigsaw piece was enough to ruin a whole puzzle. One broken wheel was enough to wreck a truck. And he always knew which toy to go for. He could sense straightaway which model was most precious, which teddy was most loved, and he would home in on it with a hatred as fierce as a laser. For it was not for the pleasure of breaking toys themselves that he did it. No, his delight was in the tears that their owners would shed. Oh such a thrill, to cause so much distress by doing so little!

But most contemptible of all was that this repulsive creature - this master of malice, this specialist in spitefulness - was himself a complete coward. He would never face his young victims. He would never risk his skin by dancing in front of them and taunting 'Look what I have done!' No, the most he ever did was to spy from the shadows. But often, by the time they discovered the damage, he was gone.

Even Mr Patchett had never actually seen the Toybreaker with his own eyes. But he had been nearer to him than almost anybody else. What he told Jamie was a story that had happened in another town, a long way from there, years and years ago.

'I was a young man at the time,' he said, as Jamie settled on a stool to listen. 'I was working for an old toe-legged boymaker.' (He meant a bow-legged toymaker, Jamie realised. He was getting the hang of it now). 'He was famous for his puppets and his theatres. People came from all over the world to buy them. He never made the same thing twice. Every puppet different.

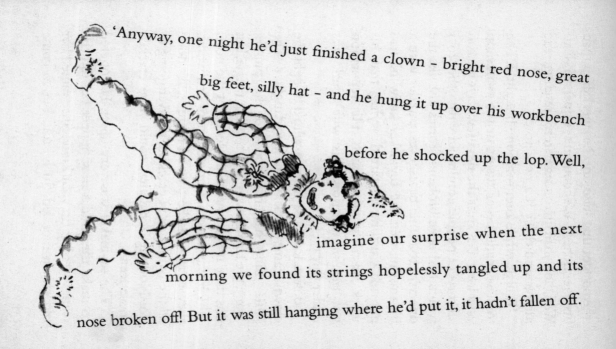

‘Anyway, one night he’d just finished a clown – bright red nose, great big feet, silly hat – and he hung it up over his workbench before he shocked up the lop. Well, imagine our surprise when the next morning we found its strings hopelessly tangled up and its nose broken off! But it was still hanging where he’d put it, it hadn’t fallen off.

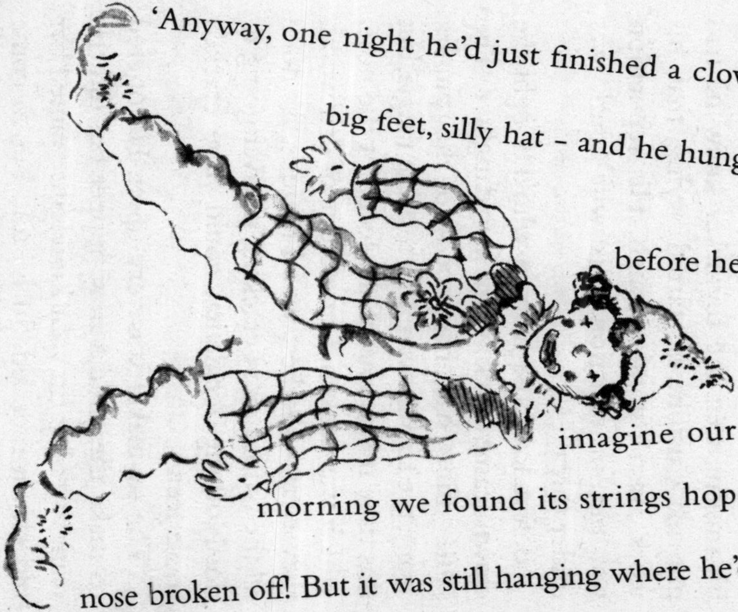

'And nothing else in the workshop had been touched. We couldn't understand it. Well, he had to completely restring the puppet and make it a new nose.

'A little while later someone bought it. The toys he made never stayed in the workshop very long. But over the next few days we had all sorts of people coming in with other toys which had been broken - stories just like the one you told me: bears' eyes, puzzles with a bit missing that the toymaker knew he had put in. Customers started saying that his work wasn't good enough. His reputation was put in question. His wife's lurk was under threat.

'Before long, the woman who'd bought the clown came back with her daughter. The same thing had happened to the puppet again: the strings were in a terrible tangle, but this time it was one of the feet, not the nose, which was broken. Carved out of driftwood, they were - the best wood there is. It's done all the twisting and cracking it's ever going to do. Nothing accidental could have cracked those feet.

'The toymaker was very upset. He offered to make the child a new puppet but did she want that? Lot on your knife! She wanted her old clown mended. So he told her to come back the next day. He carved a new share of poos and painted them, while I did the restringing. That night, the toymaker slept on a couch in the workshop. And that's how he found out about the Toybreaker.'

'Did he see him?' asked Jamie.

'Oh yes, he saw him all right. Nearly caught him. A rattling sound woke him in the middle of the night. His eyes went straight to the puppet hanging over the bench. At first nothing seemed to be moving. Then he spotted a skinny sort of shape reaching down to it from above. He flicked on the light, leapt up and was on the Toybreaker almost before he could see what it was. It wasn't very big, but its eyes filled him with cheer.'

'With cheer?' said Jamie.

'No no,' said the toymender. 'They chilled him with fear. He was frightened it might bite him, but it simply thrashed its arms and legs about, squealing all the time as he tried to get hold of it. But it was too slippery, he couldn't. He managed to grab its long, ratty tail though, as it escaped.'

'What happened?'

'The tail came off in his hand, like a lizard's. And the Toybreaker disappeared doubting in the shark.'

'The shark?' said Jamie.

'Not the shark, the dark,' said the toymender. 'Shouting in the dark.'

There was a silence, then Jamie asked:

'And was that the end of it?'

'Yes. There were no other incidents after that. The toymaker had proved too good a match for him. We assumed he'd run away to nurse his wounds. The tail soon withered to a little string. And that was the last I heard of him – until you came in just as I was about to close for supper.'

'Oh crikey!' said Jamie, jumping off the stool. 'Supper! I'm supposed to be getting fish and chips! Is there a chippie somewhere near here?'

'Yes. There's a ship chop just round the corner.'

Jamie said goodbye and dashed off, promising to come back again soon. Twice he nearly took the wrong turning. Everything looked different going in this direction. But then everything seemed different now anyway.

His heart pounded as he waited in the delicious, steamy warmth of the chip shop. What he'd heard was almost too frightening – but it was exciting as well. As soon as he had the hot, vinegar smelling parcel in his hands,

he ran back down the road,
took the first right,
the first left, followed
the narrow lane
that wound past a printer's,
through a passageway,
up some steps, down an alley, round a corner,
out onto the main street,
over the
pedestrian
crossing
and along the road that led him home.

6
Beans

Jamie couldn't wait to tell them at school. The minute he was through the gates, he began. Bringing news that nobody else knows about makes you feel important, even if it's bad news. Within minutes a crowd had collected round him, like iron filings round a magnet. This time the playground looked like this:

Matthew A.
Robby Ben Lionel
Terry
Michael Vikki
Katy Ndeye Liddy Solomon Sandra
Lizzy Winston Jonathan Simon Alice Roxanne
Natasha Matthew M. **Jamie** Wayne Cathy
Anne-Marie Thomas Samantha William
Giles Helen Ludovic Louise Myriam Becky
Christine Jeremy Emma Andrea Jason Brett
Marcus Tom Martin Bobby

It was rather satisfying to see that even the ones who had been nastiest to him before couldn't resist coming to see what all the fuss was about. It wasn't often that Jamie was the centre of attention. He decided to make the most of it.

'I know who's been breaking everything,' he announced. 'He's a sort of horrible little fiend who does it just for fun.'

'For fun?' Samantha thought of her teddy and burst into tears. This attracted even more onlookers.

'He sneaks in when no one's looking and slides away under doors or through cracks in the wall,' Jamie went on.

'Who says?' piped up Liddy.

'You're just making it up!' jeered someone from the back of the crowd.

'Oh no I'm not!' said Jamie. 'I was told it by someone who knows. So there!'

'Who?' called Giles, a boy with cotton wool sticking out of his ears. (It was because he had something wrong with them, but it looked as if the stuffing was coming out of his head.)

'A person who mends toys, that's who,' said Jamie. 'Called Mr Patchett.'

'How does he know?' sneered Thomas.

'Because the same thing happened years ago somewhere else,' Jamie told them.

'Where?' asked Matthew.

'I don't know,' said Jamie, wishing he did. He could tell that they didn't believe him. A few of them were beginning to drift away from the edge of the circle. The magnet was losing its strength. Only a couple of children still stared, with their mouths hanging open like guppies.

'But I can tell you what he's called,' said Jamie. 'He's called the Toybreaker!'

'Wow!' went Alice.

'Is he magic?' asked Wayne.

Jamie could tell that some of them were waiting for the answer just to be able to make fun of it. And it wasn't much comfort to have people like Wayne willing to believe you. Wayne would have believed you if you told him your mother was a gorilla.

'I don't know whether he's magic,' he said. He could tell that the teasers were disappointed. Nothing to get their teeth into. But why should he care? Jamie realised he didn't know enough about the Toybreaker to convince them. For a moment he was tempted to spice it up with his own imagination, but what was the point?

'If you don't believe me,' he said, 'come and meet Mr Patchett yourselves.'

Out of the corner of his eye, he could see Liddy getting ready to say something scornful about his story. But she didn't get the chance this time. The bell rang and everyone headed inside for a lesson of science.

In the spring Miss Clement had doled out a bean and a piece of blotting paper to each child in the class. She'd told them to take them home, line a jam jar with the blotting paper, slip the bean between the paper and the glass, then water it and watch the bean grow. There were twenty-nine children in the class. Two weeks later no two beans looked the same.

Some had grown neatly out of the jar and spread two perfect leaves as if to say: 'Who's a good bean then?'

Some had forced out a couple of sickly roots, gone soggy and shrivelled up.

Some had burst into an explosion of growth, filled the jar with a web of writhing roots, and shot out a tall, lanky stalk which promptly flopped over, turned blue and died.

Others had just sat there in the jar, as hard as a pebble, refusing to show the slightest sign of life.

The reason I'm talking about beans is because it was just the same with the account of the Toybreaker that each child took away with them at the end of the day.

Some watered it with their imagination till it woke them up screaming in the night. Alice's dad leapt out of bed like a jack-in-the-box, thinking there must be a burglar in her room, Alice was so scared.

With others, like Samantha and Matthew, it took root slowly but surely, till they found themselves starting to believe in it.

Others, like Liddy, considered it a complete non-starter. Jamie had broken her snowstorm, and however many other strange things may have happened, she wasn't going to believe any story *he* came up with!

As for their parents, of course, most of them had no time for talk of a Toybreaker. Take Samantha's dad: slow, methodical Mr Gorp. Would he believe in the Toybreaker? You might as well ask him to fly!

'Well where else can Albert's eye have gone?' asked Samantha.

'It's here somewhere,' her father insisted with infuriating patience. 'We just haven't found it yet.'

'But we've looked everywhere!' cried Samantha.

Mr Gorp couldn't deny this. In his search for the missing eye he'd discovered places he didn't even know existed. He'd spent an unpleasant afternoon with his finger stuck in the plughole of the bath. He'd had to take up the floorboards under the stairs again after realising that he'd nailed them back with his torch underneath.

And worst of all, after spotting what he'd thought was teddy's eye in the rubbish,

he'd groped up to his armpits through the slimy,
stinking contents of the dustbin. In
vain he'd plunged his fingers into
the mess of damp teabags, of
blackening banana peel, of fish
skin, bacon rinds and meat fat,
of soggy cereals, sticky wrappers
and rotting fruit, of snotty
tissue, chicken
carcass and festering
leftovers of every kind.

The eye that stared up at him turned out to belong to a fish skeleton. But still he wouldn't hear of any other explanation. The eye had to be there somewhere, and if they looked for long enough, they'd find it.

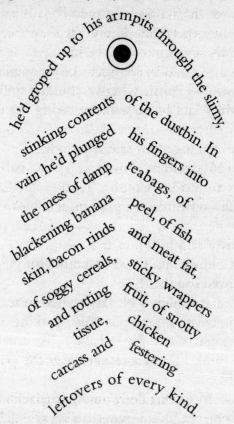

In the MacFaddles' house, Matthew and his parents sat in a row on the sofa, in front of the telly, with their supper on their laps. (It wasn't that they particularly wanted to watch anything. It was just that the dining table was covered in a half-made jigsaw of pine forests.)

'It would explain why we couldn't find it,' said Mrs MacFaddle, without taking her eyes off the screen.

'It all fits together,' said Matthew.

Mr MacFaddle shoved a great ball of spaghetti into his mouth.

'Mnliomp mnliamp pliar plior schlorp,' he said.

'What?' said his wife.

Her husband finished munching and swallowed loudly.

'I said, it sounds a bit far-fetched to me.'

'You never know,' she said, sucking in a stray spaghetti that flipped about like a netted eel. 'I think I'll put a blanket over the puzzle tonight, just in case.'

'Blollom flaefen flolly,' said Mr MacFaddle, which meant 'Better safe than sorry.'

Meanwhile, all over town, toys continued to be broken.

Wayne's baby brother Boris had a train set – a very simple train set, like this:

It was just a circle, with no junctions and no sidings, nothing complicated at all – a bit like Boris himself. He spent ages making engine noises and pushing his train round. He pushed first in one direction, then in the other. This kept him happy as a breeze for hours.

and round and round and round and round and round and round and round and round and round and round and round and round and round and round and round and round and round and round and round

Then one morning Boris found the front wheel of the engine broken. He was inconsolable. For the rest of that day he refused to budge from the middle of the train track. He ate there, he had his nappy changed there, he fell asleep there. That's where his brother found him, clutching the broken engine, when he got home. And although putting two and two together was a major operation for Wayne, he soon realised - with a shiver of excitement - that now his life too had been touched by the Toybreaker.

Most of the Toybreaker's victims were new. But there was one house he went back to for a second time - someone who had so many toys, such expensive toys, that he simply couldn't resist it. And guess who that was!

Yes, you're right. It was Liddy.

Her father, Mr Grabham-Popham (GP to his friends), was talking on his mobile phone at the breakfast bar, with an important-looking newspaper folded in his hand, and was just wondering which car to drive to work, when Liddy came panting into the kitchen.

'Daddy! My Japanese doll's broken!'

'Don't worry, honey,' he told her with a wink. 'I'll buy you another one at the airport.'

'But you said you got it from a toymaker in Tokyo.'

'I did? Well, em . . . Listen, Matt, can I call you back? We've got a bit of a blip here. Sure. Will do. Bye.' He turned to Liddy, narrowed his eyes and squared his jaw - as much as someone who has no chin can hope to. 'Now give me the facts,' he said, pointing at her.

Liddy told him that she'd found the doll on

the floor with its head broken off. Mr Grabham-Popham always knew who to blame. 'It's that cat!' he said. 'It's gotta be that cat!'

Liddy didn't question her father's verdict. He was a man of the world. He knew what was what.

'I hate that cat!' she screamed and rushed off to punish it.

The poor, fat, overfed animal was asleep (it nearly always was) in the conservatory. It didn't stay asleep for long. I won't tell you what Liddy did to it because I'd be accused by millions of animal lovers of unkindness to cats – as if it were me who'd done it! But I will tell you that when it picked itself up out of the flowerbed and stretched to check that all four of its legs were still properly joined on, it decided that the time had come to do something.

They say that cats have no conscience. And it's true that they can do the most disgusting things and not seem to feel that they're in the wrong. But they have a very strong sense of outrage if someone wrongs *them*. Liddy's cat (whose name, by the way, was Jasper) had already been suspected of breaking her snowstorm. He soon discovered what he was accused of having broken this time. And with all his cattish cunning he was determined to find out who was to blame if it should ever happen again. Which is why going back to the same house twice was the Toybreaker's first mistake.

7
A Plan of Action

Two days later, a group of eight children, led by Jamie, turned up at the toymender's. There was Tom and Samantha, Alice and Wayne, Matthew, Giles and Natasha. The toymender was terribly flustered to see so many children swarming into his workshop. The children were pretty surprised too.

Jamie suddenly realised he hadn't told them anything about Mr Patchett himself. He hadn't prepared them to expect a rather glum-looking man who mixed up his words. At least his coat looked a bit cleaner today, Jamie thought. Then he realised it was because he'd got it on inside out.

Sometimes it's only when you take someone else to see a place you like, that you realise all the things that are wrong with it or odd about it. That's how Jamie felt now, as the others glanced at each other and tried to smother grins and giggles.

It didn't help that the toymender had a great big plaster on his chin.

'Did you hurt yourself?' asked Jamie.

'What?' said the toymender. 'Oh that! No, I just shut myself caving.'

The children looked puzzled.

'He cut himself shaving,' Jamie explained. Then, turning to Mr Patchett, he said: 'I've brought some of my friends. I told them what you said about the Toybreaker and we want to try and stop him.'

He introduced Samantha, who produced her one-eyed bear out of a bag, and Tom, who held out a box containing his broken galleon.

While the toymender examined the evidence, the children peered around the cluttered room which was dimly lit by a single bare bulb.

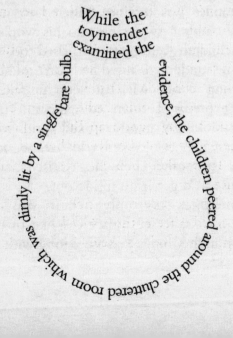

'I'm afraid it bears his hallmark,' said the toymender. 'Dear oh dear, I really hoped I'd been the sack of him.'

'Seen the back of him,' Jamie murmured to the others.

'We must stop him!' cried Giles heroically.

'Yes!' piped up Alice. 'I'll help.'

'Easier dead than sun,' sighed the toymender.

'*I* know,' suggested Tom. 'We could catch him in a net!'

'Or we could spread out a patch of glue so that he'd get his feet stuck in it!' said Samantha.

'No,' said Matthew. 'A poisoned sweet would be better!'

'Why not just zap him with a laser gun?' said Jonathan.

'Woh!' said the toymender. 'You're putting the heart before the course. The first thing we've got to decide isn't how we're going to catch him. You're quite right, of course, that we've got to tray a good lap. But the question is: where? We can't be everywhere at once. The Toybreaker could strike almost anywhere.'

'He hasn't been to my house yet!' volunteered Alice enthusiastically.

'I shouldn't be so keen about it,' said

Samantha. 'You won't like it when he does.'

'All right, all right. Calm down,' said the toymender, a little irritably. 'It's best to go up a ladder one tongue at a rhyme.'

'You mean: one rung at a time,' said Tom.

'That's what I said,' snapped the toymender. 'Now, let me see, last time this happened, it was in the cop that we nearly short him.'

The children looked at each other but didn't say anything. The more agitated he got, the more mistakes he seemed to make. He went on:

'I think he must have hated the idea that something he'd broken was being put right again.'

'Could you mend Samantha's bear? Or Tom's boat?' asked Jamie.

'I could,' said the toymender, 'if they wanted me to. But I'd have to barge them for the chits.'

Wayne looked puzzled. Matthew whispered to him.

'It's worth a try,' said Jamie to Tom and Samantha. Both of them agreed to the plan. The toymender would fix the broken toys, leave them in his workshop, and they'd set a trap to try and catch the Toybreaker when he came.

They spent the next half hour deciding what

exactly the trap would consist of. The ideas ranged from the unpromising to the impossible, from the meticulous to the ridiculous. Here's what they ended up with:

1 **A sheet** spread over the workbench, on which the repaired toys would sit. The corners of the sheet would be attached to strings so that the whole thing could be hoisted up suddenly with the Toybreaker inside it.

2 **A net** suspended above the workbench, which could be released by a tug on another string. This would fall over the hoisted sheet to stop the Toybreaker scrambling out.

3 **A strip** of wood that could be swung under the door to prevent him from sliding out that way.

'I'll need someone else to help me with the white notch,' said the toymender. 'We can't afford to miss him, so we'll have to weigh a steak all night.'

Jamie said he'd be willing to stay up, though he'd have to ask his mum. So did Alice. The toymender promised to repair the bear and the galleon straightaway.

'Saturday night then,' he told them, as they made their way to the door. 'And remember – it's a secret. He won't come if he hears about it. So what a nerd to anyone!'

8
The Night Watch

Alice's parents said no.

Well, what did you expect? They didn't know Mr Patchett. And as for Alice's story about some weird little monster . . . Of course they said no!

Jamie waited for a moment when his mum was busy Doing It Herself. That wasn't difficult. She Did It most of the time. Right now she was struggling with the light she'd been fitting in the kitchen, which for some reason wouldn't switch off.

'Mu-um?' he began.

'Pass me the screwdriver,' she said.

'WhatwouldyousayifItoldyouthatwe'regoing totryandcatchasortofevilspritewellhe'snotasprite exactlybuthekeepsbreakingpeople'stoysand

MrPatchettthat'sthetoymenderwhohasawork shopintownknowsabouthimfrombefore andsaysthatthesamethinghappenedyearsago somewhereelsesohe'sgoingtomendacoupleof thethingthathavebeenbrokenandwe'regoingto usethemasbaitandlieinwaitforhimforthe ToybreakerImeanbecausenooneknowswhere hecomesfrombuthe'scausingmoreandmore troubleandsomeonehastodosomethingsoisitall rightifIkeepwatchonSaturdaynightwithhim?'

'Pass me the wire cutters,' she said.

'Mum,' asked Jamie, 'did you hear what I said?'

'Just a minute. I've nearly finished.'

Sometimes, getting a simple answer out of a grown-up is harder than prising a limpet off a rock. In the end, Jamie never did get a proper answer out of her. But she did agree to come along and meet 'this person,' as she called him, and see what it was all about.

So the next day they pulled the front door shut behind them (difficult, without a handle) and set off into town. It was raining.

'Mum!' said Jamie. 'You've got paint on your cheek!'

She stopped and scratched at her reflection in the butcher's window.

'That better?' she asked. It wasn't, much.

Why is it so embarrassing when your parents

look funny or say things you don't want them to say? After all, if it was someone else's mum with paint on her cheek, you'd just think: 'Oh, she's been painting.' But when it's your own mum, it's the most embarrassing thing on earth.

The rain got heavier.
It splattered on the pavements.
It dripped off their noses and hair as they hurried
through the streets to the toymender's. Jamie walked a
few paces ahead of his mum. Suddenly he remembered
how he'd felt when he took his friends to meet
Mr Patchett. 'By the way,' he said, turning
towards her, 'his workshop's a bit
of a mess.'

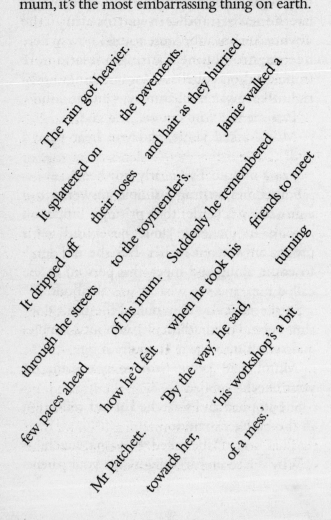

A car hissed past and sprayed the contents of a puddle all over his mum's legs. 'Oh,' he said, stopping again, 'and he tends to get his words a bit muddled up.'

A spurt of water from the roof shot straight down her neck. 'Never mind that,' she said, waving him on. 'Let's just get there!'

Jamie pushed open the door. The bell clattered. In they stepped, two bedraggled rats, bringing their own puddles with them. The toymender emerged from the back room and blinked at them. 'It's me,' said Jamie. 'And this is my mum.'

'Hello,' said the toymender, with a sort of sad smile. 'Roaring with pain, is it?' Jamie's mum looked puzzled. 'Well, you'd better dry yourselves off.'

While they rubbed themselves down with towels, Mr Patchett made some tea. Jamie's mum gazed about the workshop. She was fascinated by all the tools that hung on the walls. There were literally hundreds of them, many she couldn't even have named. The man was obviously a master craftsman. But his skill didn't appear to extend to electrical work. As she rubbed her hair, she noticed the bare bulb that dangled over the workbench.

'I could fix you up something brighter than that, if you like,' she volunteered, as the toymender brought in a teapot.

Jamie cringed, thinking of that kitchen light. His mum's electrical work was worse than her plastering. At home you couldn't use more than one appliance at a time or the fuse blew, and the bathroom heater would only work if the hall light was switched on.

'I did buy one of those striplights once but I never got round to putting it up,' Mr Patchett said. 'I'm afraid I've only got two cups. Oh dear,' he said, as he poured tea the colour of cola, 'I hope you strike it long.'

Two hours later, the rain had stopped, but Jamie and his mum were still there. She'd asked the toymender all about his work and he'd become quite perky telling her about it. Jamie had even had trouble steering the conversation back to the Toybreaker, which was, after all, the reason they had come. In the end though, his mum had agreed to spend Saturday night sitting up with them in the workshop, in the hope of catching him. She got quite excited about the trap Mr Patchett was planning to lay and – to Jamie's dismay as he thought of her D.I.Y.– added several suggestions as to how it might be improved.

'Twelve o'clock!' exclaimed the toymender. 'Can I offer you a light of bunch?'

It was mid-afternoon before they left.

'What a nice man!' said Jamie's mother as they walked home. 'Workshop could do with a bit of modernising though.' Jamie realised he needn't have worried what she'd think of Mr Patchett. But he still wished she hadn't got that speck of paint on her cheek.

On Saturday afternoon, six of the eight children who had been to meet the toymender met up again at his workshop to help lay the trap. (Jonathan had a football match and Natasha had twisted her ankle doing pirouettes in the dentist's waiting room.) Tom was delighted to see his galleon so skilfully repaired, and Samantha couldn't believe her eyes - or rather her bear's, which gazed up at her as if nothing had ever happened. How had the toymender managed to find an eye so exactly like the one that had gone missing? The trouble was, neither of them was now very keen to have their belongings used as bait to catch the Toybreaker. They couldn't bear to think of them being damaged a second time.

'But that's the whole point,' said the toymender. 'He'll hate seeing that the things he broke have been put right again. That's what we're counting on. But you don't need to worry. We'll cake tear of them.'

'Go on,' said Alice. 'It's for the sake of everyone else.'

'You wouldn't say that if you'd had something of yours spoilt,' said Samantha, clutching Albert.

But in the end they agreed to take the risk. The traps were set up. Jamie had brought the sheet. Tom had brought the net. Towards the end of the afternoon Jamie's mum turned up with a big suitcase containing, amongst other things, a cup, a sleeping bag, some electrical tools, two toothbrushes and a cake. She cut up the cake and the children munched it excitedly while they admired their work.

'What will you do with him when you've caught him?' asked Wayne.

'He ought to be punished for what he's done!' said Samantha. 'I hate him!'

'Let's cross that bridge when we come to it,' said the toymender. 'The plan may not work. You mustn't haze your ropes.'

Samantha reluctantly kissed her teddy goodbye. He looked so vulnerable, sitting there on the workbench with the net rigged up over him. Tom cast a last glance at his galleon. And then they went, leaving Jamie, his mum and the toymender to wait for nightfall.

It got dark early, being mid-November. Jamie's mum had wired up the striplight for Mr Patchett but they didn't put it on. They didn't want to give the Toybreaker any sign that they were there. For hours they sat in near darkness. Jamie's eyes got used to the different types of black that meant wall, workbench, door. To pass the time they talked, though only in low voices.

'Do you think he'll come?' said Jamie.

'We'll have to wait and see,' said the toymender.

'We won't have lost anything if he doesn't,' said his mum.

'Except a night's sleep,' said the toymender.

But Jamie knew that he had a lot to lose. If the Toybreaker didn't come, people would say he'd just been lying. They'd say he'd been leading them on. He felt a sudden urge to tell his mum and Mr Patchett how he'd been bullied at school.

'You know those toys that have been broken,' he began in a near whisper. 'People think that I did it.'

Somehow, it was easier to say it in the darkness.

'You?' said his mum. 'Whyever should they think that?'

'I don't know,' said Jamie, knowing perfectly well but not wanting to make his mum feel bad about it. 'Maybe because I haven't got all the things that they've got.

They think I did it out of spite.'

'That's ridiculous!' said his mum, raising her voice.

'Shhhh,' the toymender reminded her. 'It's unkind. It's unfair. It's untrue. But it's not ridiculous. I've known it happen once myself, way back when I was learning my trade. It was a little boy whose Mad and Dumb had both died when he was a baby and whose old uncle was left looking after him. The uncle was very poor and as a result the child had hardly any toys at all. He was terribly jealous of other children who had more. And what did he do? There was nothing he could do to the uncle who was a change old strap. People said he had magic powers. The child was frightened of him. So he took it out on the other children, by breaking their things. That's how I know about it. They'd get brought along to our workshop to be mended. Of course he tried to do it secretly, but he got found out.'

The toymender's voice had held them spellbound. When it stopped, the darkness itself seemed to be waiting for more.

'What happened to him?' Jamie asked.

'Well his uncle gave him a hood guiding, I know that. But he still carried on. In the end the child was sent away somewhere.'

'Jamie would never do a thing like that!' said his mum.

'Of course not,' said Mr Patchett. 'But that's all the more reason to try and catch the Toybreaker, so we can prove that Jamie's innocent.'

On the other side of town, in the leafy private road where Liddy lived, a shadowy shape crept across a darkened lawn. It stopped every couple of steps and froze, like a squirrel, looking anxiously around. Then it disappeared behind a tree that overhung a conservatory.

Moments later, it appeared again. It ran across the lawn without once looking back. Had it looked back, it would have seen the silhouette of a rather chubby cat loping along after it.

A clock in town chimed midnight.

A full moon floated up over the rooftops and poured its light through the dirty windows of the shop, laying two rows of silver tiles on the floor.

Above them, dust swirled and circled endlessly in the moonbeams. Jamie watched it for a while, mesmerised.

'It's weird to think the air's full of dust like that all the time and we're not even aware of it,' he said.

'There's a lot going on that we're not aware of,' said the toymender.

They could see each other faintly now. Jamie could just make out the shapes on the workbench: the pale presence of the galleon, the teddy's eyes glinting in the gloom. Every now and then he reached down to check the two strings that lay at his feet - the strings that would hoist up the sheet and release the net. It was Mr Patchett who had given him this job. That just left his mum to switch on the light, and Mr Patchett to swing the strip of wood under the door.

Time passed. They were all feeling sleepy.

Then Jamie heard a strange hissing sound, like air escaping from a balloon.

'Listen!' he said, sitting up in his chair.

Everyone listened but they couldn't hear anything. A few minutes later it happened again.

'It's only Mr Patchett yawning,' said Jamie's mum, whose own eyes kept wanting to close.

'I need something to weep me a cake,' said the toymender.

'I'm afraid it's all gone,' said Jamie's mum.

'What has?'

'The cake.'

'No, I was thinking of a cup of tea,' he said. So without putting on the lights, he got up and made a pot of tea.

But even after the tea Jamie's mum could hardly keep her eyes open.

'Why don't you take a little rest?' the toymender suggested. 'Jamie and I can keep watch. It's too much to expect anyone to stay on their nose all tight.'

So his mum wriggled into the sleeping bag she had brought and fell asleep in the armchair. It was very kind of Mr Patchett to have suggested it because he was extremely sleepy himself. In fact, soon afterwards, Jamie heard him snoring. 'What if the Toybreaker struck now?' Jamie thought.

'Mum,' he hissed, giving her a nudge. 'Mum!' But she wouldn't wake up. So Jamie sat there in the dark between the two sleeping grown-ups, feeling distinctly cold, and waited.

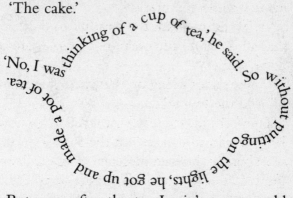

Meanwhile, up above the narrow streets where the workshop was, a strange creature scuttled over the rooftops in the moon-light, confident that up there nobody would see him.

Jamie yawned. Was there really all this time in every night, he wondered. The town clock struck one, then two.

Then suddenly, he heard something – a rustling noise coming from the direction of the back room. His heart started beating like a bass drum. He strained his eyes but couldn't see anything moving. Trying not to make any sudden movement himself, he reached out his hand and gave his mother a prod. She let out a sigh and turned over. Jamie held his breath and listened. For a moment there was nothing. Then, loud in the silence, he heard a scraping sound. Jamie tried shaking his mum. He was getting desperate. He leant over and gave the toymender several urgent taps on the shoulder.

Mr Patchett woke with a start as a squeal and a hiss came from the workbench. He shot out his legs and sent the teapot flying with a great clatter across the floor. Jamie tugged on both strings. At the same moment his mum leapt to her feet and reached for the light switch. In the first flash of light they saw the net falling onto the gathered-up sheet. All three of them sprang forward. Jamie's mum, forgetting she was still in a sleeping bag, keeled over with a shriek. The toymender went tumbling over her. In the next flash Jamie saw what looked like two shapes darting from the workbench. What should he do? His mum, desperately trying to get out of the sleeping bag, was writhing on the floor like a stabbed caterpillar. Meanwhile, instead of coming on properly, the light kept flickering on and off like something at a disco.

'Where is he?' said Jamie anxiously, grabbing the empty sheet.

As the grown-ups stumbled to their feet, a door banged in the back room.

'Blast!' said the toymender. 'I didn't think about the cellar! Quick!'

In the flashing light, they followed him into the back room where he opened a door Jamie had never noticed before. He led them down a narrow staircase into a cellar whose air seemed to clutch you with its coldness. It was full of old boxes and dusty stacks of wood. Another bare bulb hung from the ceiling.

'Shhhh!' said the toymender, though no one was making a noise. Jamie could feel his mum's breath on his neck. He peered all round the room. If someone was hiding, they were keeping very still. Now, for the first time, Jamie felt frightened. The Toybreaker could be anywhere here. How did they know he wouldn't do something vicious to them? Animals often turned dangerous when they were trapped.

Jamie found himself holding his breath, as if he'd be able to hear better without the noise of his own breathing. But no sound broke the silence. Mr Patchett took a step forward. Jamie's eyes darted nervously from one pile of clutter to the next. There were a hundred hiding places here. Not knowing where the creature was - perhaps even being watched by him at this moment - Jamie felt as if he, and not the Toybreaker, were the one who was being hunted. All at once, a piece of wood slipped in one corner. Everyone's heart leapt. The toymender seized a stick and jabbed it behind the stack of planks. Suddenly something sprang out with a yowl, shot past them and hurtled away up the stairs.

But it was only a cat - a fat, frightened, fluffed up cat - just like the one that Jamie had seen at Liddy's.

The toymender looked at the other two, sighed, and turned to go back up the steps.

'No, wait,' said Jamie. 'I'm sure I saw him upstairs.' He felt close to tears. His mum put her arm round him.

'It was just a cat,' she said. 'We all saw it with our own eyes.'

Five hours later, in the grey light of morning, Jamie and his mum stood on the toymender's step saying goodbye. After the false alarm, they'd set up the trap again and taken turns at keeping watch, but nothing else had happened. His mum promised to call back the next day to try and get the light working.

They trudged back through the deserted, Sunday streets, his mum carrying the suitcase she'd brought, Jamie with a box containing the repaired bear and galleon to return to Matthew and Samantha.

'I know what they're going to say,' he said.

'Look, you've done your best,' his mum told him. Then with a grin she added: 'What door can you moo?' And they both laughed.

9
Doubts

'What did you expect?' said Liddy for the tenth time. A crowd of children pressed around her in the playground. 'It's all nonsense, this Toybreaker stuff!'

'*I* believe it,' said Wayne.

'You believe in the Easter Bunny!' said Liddy, contemptuously. 'And as for grown-ups believing in it . . .!' she added loudly, to make sure that Jamie would hear.

'How do you know that this toymender believes it?' asked Jonathan.

'Don't be silly,' said Alice. 'It was him who told Jamie about it in the first place.'

'That doesn't necessarily mean he believes in it,' said Jonathan, with a cunning look in his eyes.

'Anyway, he wouldn't sit up all night

waiting to catch something he didn't believe in, would he?' said Tom.

'He might do,' said Jonathan, 'if he wanted *us* to believe in it.'

'What are you getting at?' asked Samantha.

'Doesn't it seem a bit fishy to you,' said Jonathan, 'that this toymender managed to find an eye exactly like the one her bear had lost?'

'What do you mean?' asked Matthew with the horrible feeling that he already knew.

'Well,' said Jonathan, 'maybe he's in league with the Toybreaker! Maybe he deliberately sends him out to break things - or take things! After all, you said he'd complained about not having much work. Maybe he's the Toybreaker himself!'

There were gasps and whispers. Shivers went down several spines. Even Jamie got a nasty, hollow feeling in his stomach when he heard it. It was a thought that had never occurred to him. How he wished he had never got mixed up in it all! How he wished he had never told them anything about the toymender! How he wished he had never even met him!

Soon afterwards the bell rang. They all funnelled into their rooms. Of Class Seven, Liddy marched in first,

Michael Vikki Marcus Tom Martin
Helen Ludovic Louise Ben
followed by Bobby Jason Brett
Matthew A. Lionel Wayne Cathy
Terry Robby Katy Ndeye Liddy
Jonathan Solomon Sandra Lizzy Winston
Simon Alice Roxanne Natasha
Matthew M. Christine Jeremy Emma Andrea
Samantha William Anne-Marie Giles Thomas
Myriam Becky

and on his own, at the back, Jamie. He wished he didn't have to go in at all. If he'd known what was coming, he probably wouldn't have done.

Miss Clement stood in her droopy cardigan at the front of the class looking solemn.

'It has come to my notice,' she began, 'that some people have been behaving very unkindly.' In the silence, she looked from one person to another with those big, disappointed eyes that made you feel guilty even if you hadn't done anything. 'Now I know there have been a lot of unfortunate incidents with broken toys lately, but that's no reason to victimise someone. Who can tell me what "victimise" means?'

Several hands shot up. They belonged to those goody-goodies who believed that if they could answer it, they'd be joining Miss Clement's side. Jamie knew what it meant all right but he didn't put up his hand. Miss Clement had heard what had been going on. Some of the children had told her about the Toybreaker too. You can imagine the scene:

Miss Clement
standing behind her desk
at the front of the class.

Jonathan sitting with his chin on his fists, staring into space.

Samantha biting her lip and fiddling with her fingernails.

Giles poking at an itch in his nose that wouldn't go away.

Tom hunched over and watching Jamie out of the corner of his eye.

Wayne trying hard to concentrate, with his mouth hanging wide open.

Alice sucking her thumb and sulking, looking into her lap.

Matthew frowning, with his hands in his pockets, his legs stuck out in front of him.

Jamie not daring to look at anyone, sure they were all looking at him.

The lecture went on for what seemed like hours. When it was over, everyone had a numb bottom and was dying to get up and move about. But instead of letting them do that, Miss Clement said she wanted them to write either a story or a poem about someone who was blamed for something they hadn't done.

You might think Jamie should have been able to do this without any problem, being, as it were, an expert in it. But however much he tried to concentrate, his mind was too full of other things. After half an hour he had only written the barest beginning of a story. He wondered:

if I wrote out
the first few
lines in a
funny way,
will that
make
it into
poetry

?

He tried it. It seemed to keep Miss Clement happy.

When he got home, he found the door handle fixed and the front door locked. Jamie was impressed, until his mum admitted that she couldn't unlock it and that he'd have to climb in through the window.

'How was today?' she asked.

'All right,' said Jamie. That's what he always said.

'Have you thought what you'd like for Christmas?' she said, casually.

Jamie was amazed. It was true that Christmas was only five or six weeks away, but normally he didn't expect to get anything much, least of all to be asked what he'd like.

'I don't know,' he said. 'Why? Have you won the lottery or something?'

'No,' said his mum. 'I just wondered.'

But somehow the question kept coming back to him. He allowed himself to imagine all the things he'd ask for if they had more money – a bike, for example. But thoughts like that only left a bad taste in his mouth – a taste of envy, a taste of anger at the unfairness of the world. He remembered that phrase that Miss Clement had used – 'those less fortunate than ourselves' – and reflected that for the likes of Liddy that meant just about everybody. She'd also warned them against believing stories that they heard, about learning to tell the difference between fantasy and reality. Did she really believe it was that easy?

Poor Jamie didn't know what to think. As he lay in bed that night, his head turned. His mind was in a spin. A hundred questions battered him like waves breaking on the rocks. Could Mr Patchett be on the Toybreaker's side? Wouldn't that explain how the Toybreaker had known where to go?

But if he knew there was a trap, why had he come? Had he come? Or was it only that cat after all? But hadn't Jamie seen two shapes escaping? Why hadn't he spent longer looking in the cellar? He tried to slow his thoughts down but he was caught in a whirlpool. What if Jonathan was right and it was his own envy making all these things happen? What if Liddy was right? What if the toymender was completely mad? How come Jamie had so readily trusted him? But hadn't his mum believed the toymender as well? Or had she just gone along with it to keep Jamie happy? How did you ever know who to trust? Why should you trust anyone? How could you know the truth about anything? How? Why? What if? Surges of doubt, swells of suspicion, flung him one way then the other. Jamie felt he was drowning in a sea of uncertainty.

10
One Thing After Another

Samantha arrived home to find her father, the baggy-faced Mr Gorp, on his hands and knees in the gutter in front of their house. The rest of the family were standing round him. Her little brother was crying. His favourite toy was an old-fashioned clockwork car that had to be wound up with a key. He'd been playing with it on the pavement the day before and now the key was missing. Mr Gorp had decided to look for it outside.

'Well, it's not in the gutter,' he said. 'But there's one other possibility.'

'What would that be?' asked his wife, adoringly.

Mr Gorp pointed to the drain.

'What, you mean . . .?'

'Precisely,' said her husband. 'It could have

been washed down by the rain. Freddy, roll up my sleeves.'

Five minutes later, the drain cover lay to one side and Mr Gorp lay stretched out with one flabby cheek pressed to the pavement and one arm plunged into the foul-smelling hole. His fingers fished blindly in the black sludge at the bottom and pulled out a number of slimy twigs, a decomposing glove, a dead frog, and various lumps of matter as unrecognisable as they were revolting. Needless to say, he did not find the key.

Samantha rushed up to her room to make sure that Albert was all right. He was lying peacefully on the bed. She picked him up and looking into his face, asked, 'Is it him again? Is it the Toybreaker?' It made her shudder to think that one of those kindly, brown eyes had actually seen the Toybreaker at work. 'If only you could talk!' Samantha said.

Over the next few days the list of broken toys and missing parts got longer and longer.

A
doll's
house
which Alice treasured above
everything else was found with its
hinges broken so that the whole front no
longer swung smoothly to reveal the cosy rooms inside. Instead, it scraped on the floor and had to be hitched up before it would close. This upset all the little pots and ornaments, vases and bottles on the tiny shelves, and jerked all the furniture out of place. It was the perfect neatness of the doll's house that Alice loved so much and to have it all in a mess like this just broke her heart. A door, a window, a table or chair - anything else could have been mended or replaced, but this had damaged the very nature of the house itself. Alice knew it would never be the same.

And then there was Jonathan - clever, inquisitive Jonathan. He'd never thought he would be targeted by the Toybreaker. He had no bears. He didn't play with railways or cars. The kind of toys that Jonathan enjoyed were complicated electronic games.

Remember what I said about the Toybreaker's delight in causing as much damage as he could with as little effort as possible? Well, although he knew next to nothing about electronics, he did know that one chip at a microchip, one scratch to a microcircuit, could stop a whole device from working. And what was so gloriously satisfying was that – because it was so complex and so small – it was virtually impossible to see where the damage had been done! A Toybreaker's dream!

Jonathan tapped on the buttons incredulously for some time before he had to admit that something was wrong.

And even then it didn't occur to him straight away that it may not have gone wrong all on its own. But when the thought of the Toybreaker passed like a shadow across his mind, he felt a chill that changed his view of everything.

By now, more than ten children had had their favourite toys broken. Although some of them still thought that the toymender might have something to do with it, no one seriously suspected Jamie any more. And in spite of the failure of their plan to catch the culprit, no one really doubted that the Toybreaker was to blame. No one, that is, except Liddy.

Perhaps it wasn't just because Liddy had so many toys that the Toybreaker felt drawn to her. Perhaps he wasn't convinced that he'd found her favourite one, and even after two attempts didn't feel he'd struck where it hurt most. Maybe that was why he had come back for a third go, the same night he had been to Mr Patchett's and had that narrow escape with the cat. But precisely because Liddy had so many things, it was a couple of days before she even discovered what he had broken this time.

Liddy's theatre had been made especially for her. The front was beautifully decorated in reds and golds, while the stage was a storehouse of different scenes, from palace to prison, from cottage to fairytale castle.

But it was none of these that the Toybreaker had damaged.

These could have been thrown out or replaced.

What he went for was the thing that gave the whole theatre its mystery, the thing that – beautiful in itself – hid, then revealed, the secret of the scenery.

The curtains of Liddy's theatre were its crowning glory.

They were made of red velvet and, by means of a clever mechanism that Liddy had never understood, they swept upwards and aside, perfectly together, when you turned a little wheel. Yet they never disappeared out of sight.

While you marvelled at each miniature world, they hung there, gathered up on each side, as if to remind you that everything could vanish again as magically as it had come. And now, these magnificent curtains were jammed, neither properly open nor properly closed.

'What were you doing to it, poppet?' asked Mrs Grabham-Popham.

'I wasn't doing anything to it,' said Liddy.

'You must have been doing *something*,' her mother insisted.

'I tell you I wasn't!' said Liddy, stamping her foot.

Mrs Grabham-Popham was usually sympathetic to her spoilt daughter. But her husband, who bought her everything she wanted, was in New York on business and had just phoned up to say that he'd be away for a few days longer than expected, and so wouldn't be able to take her out to dinner and to the theatre as they'd planned. As a result, she was feeling deeply sorry for herself and had very little sympathy left for Liddy.

'Where's the cat?' Liddy asked.

'In the conservatory,' said Mrs Grabham-Popham.

'I thought we agreed not to let him in!' said Liddy.

'I hardly think he could have done that,'

said her mother, who was beginning to get a little tired of Liddy's broken toys. 'You'll have to wait for your father to come home. He'll know what to do.'

Now, as a matter of fact, Jasper the cat had been quite pleased with his success in tracking down and attacking the Toybreaker a few nights before. He'd ended up getting cornered himself, admittedly, but still he'd given the Toybreaker a good fright. And since no one had accused Jasper of breaking anything, and Mrs Grabham-Popham had even let him back in the house again, he'd assumed he was out of danger. So it came as a sleep-shattering, fur-raising shock when Liddy suddenly flew at him in another tantrum without warning. Sitting outside afterwards in the wet grass, giving himself a good wash, Jasper decided that the time had come to prove his innocence once and for all. But how could he do it?

If only he knew it, Jasper was soon to get his chance.

When Liddy got to school the next day she was amazed to hear so many children telling stories about broken toys. What's more, when Miss Clement came into the playground, they all clustered around her to tell her about it.

Miss Clement listened. What they described was certainly puzzling. She quite understood how upsetting it was. But she couldn't bring herself to believe in all this Toybreaker business. Which is what, in as kindly a way as possible, she told them.

'But, Miss,' said Jonathan. 'It's happened to so many people, it can't just be a coincidence.'

'It's getting worse and worse,' said Samantha.

'And with Christmas coming up, it could be terrible!' squeaked Alice.

Miss Clement took her responsibilities very seriously. She couldn't just brush off their concern like so many of their parents had. So when Jonathan suggested setting up an experiment in class to see whether the Toybreaker would come, Miss Clement felt it was only fair to go along with it. It seemed to her like a good way of proving to them that - unfortunate though all this was - there was nothing mysterious about it after all.

The plan was this: the children would spend the afternoon finishing the model castle they had been building out of matches and lolly sticks, then they'd leave the top window open overnight to entice the Toybreaker into the classroom. Surely something they had spent so much time and effort on would be too much for him to resist. If it was broken the next morning, they'd have conclusive proof that he existed.

Liddy felt uneasy about the plan. She hated the idea of ever having to admit that she was wrong. She told her mother about it that afternoon, while the cat watched warily from its chair. Though she didn't know it, Jasper was listening carefully to every word. Mrs Grabham-Popham, even though she thought most primary teachers were rather silly and childish, was surprised at Miss Clement's going this far. But she was too busy feeling husbandless to worry about it for long.

And what about Jamie? We haven't mentioned him for a while. How did he feel about all this? Nothing of his had been broken, and he knew that he wouldn't be getting the kind of flashy Christmas presents that would be likely to attract the Toybreaker. He should have been pleased, shouldn't he, that most of them now believed what he'd said? He should have felt relieved that he was no longer under suspicion. He should have felt glad that he'd stepped out of the spotlight and that it was now his teacher who had taken the matter up. But the main thing Jamie felt was just unsettled. Ever since that night when his mind had been a whirlpool of worries, he'd been aware of a strange, nervous feeling inside him, as if someone were watching all the time. Even as he withdrew into the background and left it to the others to say what they thought, Jamie felt - and it turned out to be right - that he was somehow still at the very centre of things.

11
In the News

That evening Jamie told his mum about the experiment they had set up to tempt the Toybreaker.

'Well,' said his mum, 'I hope they have more luck than we did. Staying up all night to catch a cat wasn't my idea of fun. By the way,' she said, 'what would you say if we invited Mr Patchett to have Christmas dinner with us? It seems a shame for him to be all on his own at Christmas.'

Jamie thought it was a nice idea. Like most children, he looked forward to Christmas. He enjoyed it when the lights were put up in town. He liked the glitter and colour of the shop window displays. He didn't even mind the flood of adverts on television for toys and games that he knew they'd never be able to afford. But most of all he loved the Christmas tree - carrying it home, decorating it, then having the sight and piney smell of it in the house throughout the Christmas holidays.

But perhaps no one looked forward to Christmas as eagerly as the Toybreaker. Alice had been right: for him it was the perfect time to strike - new toys everywhere, surprises to be spoilt. Christmas for him would be a feast of havoc, a jamboree of destruction. His ears were tuned in to the hopes, the longings of a hundred children. No wonder then, that he heard about the castle just waiting to be damaged at school. No wonder too, with twenty-nine children all telling their parents about it, that he decided - after that fright at the toymender's - to keep well away.

The next morning Jamie's class could hardly wait for their classroom to be opened. Miss Clement herself didn't share their impatience. She knew that nothing would have happened to the castle. Seeing their eager faces, she almost felt sorry for them, guessing the disappointment they'd feel. She waited for them to line up. Only Liddy and Jamie remained calm: Liddy because she didn't believe in the Toybreaker, and Jamie because he'd lost hope of catching him.

Miss Clement unlocked the door and the children poured in like water through a broken dam and swirled around the table where the castle had been left. Jamie and Liddy were at the back of the crowd, so couldn't see anything at first. But Miss Clement, though still at the door, could see quite clearly over their heads and was flabbergasted by what she saw.

There were shouts, gasps. The castle had not been damaged - it had been wrecked! No part of it had escaped, from its towers and its battlements to its drawbridge and its portcullis. Every wall was smashed. Every detail was splintered or split. It looked like a real castle might have done after a violent siege.

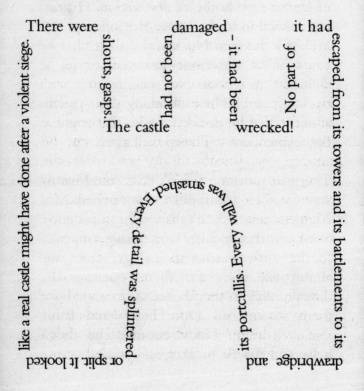

There can have been no child in the class who didn't feel that their own work had been spoilt, their own efforts wasted. Miss Clement was speechless.

As some of the children pulled away, Liddy too saw the evidence. Like her teacher, she felt as if a trap door had opened beneath her. With a kind of hollow, sinking feeling, she, too, realised that she had been wrong.

Jamie as well could see the castle now, from where he stood at the back of the room. The sight of it made him shudder. But it puzzled him too. There was something odd about it, something wild and crazy about the attack. He was glad that the experiment had worked, though. Even his teacher should believe in the Toybreaker now. Then, turning away, he noticed several marks on the glass below the small window they had left open. He glanced down and spotted one or two more on the floor. It was strange, they looked a bit like cat's pawmarks. Without quite knowing why, he checked that no one was looking, then leant on the window and rubbed his back against it. Casually as he could, he turned to make sure the pawmarks had gone. Then, dragging his foot over the ones on the floor, he wandered across to his desk.

With Miss Clement on the children's side, things moved into a new gear. The first thing she did was to go and see Mr Patchett, to hear for herself what he could tell her about the Toybreaker.

'Hello,' she said, 'I'm Kate Clement, Jamie's teacher.'

'Oh yes,' said the toymender, holding out a hand spotted with bright red paint. 'Mice to neat you. Come on in.'

Having heard what a funny, old-fashioned kind of shop he had, she was quite surprised to find the walls and ceiling all white and newly painted.

'Booking letter, isn't it?' he said. 'It's Jamie's mother actually who's been doing all this.'

Miss Clement asked if he'd mind telling her everything he'd told Jamie about the Toybreaker. For a good half hour she sat and listened, nodding and asking questions. When he had finished, she explained how anxious she was for the children's Christmas and how she was determined to do something. The toymender shook his head.

'I don't want to put you off,' he said, 'but the thing is, you're up against a formidable enemy. He's more sly and slippery than you can imagine. I mean, we tried setting a trap for him. We stayed up all night. And look where it got us. I'm afraid, when it comes to catching the Toybreaker, you're hanging your bed against a brick wall.'

'I beg your pardon?' said Miss Clement.

'I said you're banging your head against a brick wall,' the toymender thought he repeated.

'But this would be different,' said Miss Clement. 'I'm not just talking about setting the odd trap here or there. I'm talking about getting everyone involved - parents, police, the media, everyone.'

'Ah,' said Mr Patchett. 'I see. That lasts a different kite on it.'

'But the problem is,' she went on, 'all we know about him comes from you. And naturally - well, I did it myself to begin with - people are going to say it's not possible. So what I need to know is: would you be willing to speak to the press about it, or even appear yourself on television?'

There's an old saying that 'no news is good news'. This is supposed to mean that if you get no news from someone, then there's nothing to worry about, because if something had gone wrong you'd have soon heard about it. And it's true that if everything's just carrying on as usual then there's not much to say. But for newspapers and news programmes, having no news is very bad news. People don't want to buy a newspaper full of blank pages or turn on the telly and hear someone announcing that nothing much has happened today. They have to have news and the worse it is, the better!

So the story of the Toybreaker was just what they wanted. It was unusual. It was alarming. It involved children and their families (which was always a good thing). It had a special Christmas angle (which was excellent). And best of all, it was a story that would run! It wasn't just like a fire, which went out, or a burglary, that was over and done with. This story had a future! Who knew how it would develop or where it might lead? It had already caused a lot of misery and suffering and with a bit of luck it could still generate plenty more!

The local paper sent out their top reporter and photographer to talk to Samantha and her little brother. Mr Gorp, you'll remember, was much too down-to-earth to believe in the Toybreaker, but now that the newspaper people were taking it seriously, he began to change his mind. He and his wife were secretly rather proud that their children had been chosen to be interviewed.

When Samantha had told her story, the reporter asked her, 'Have you got the bear here? Can I have a look at him?' He gave a wink to the photographer, who lifted his camera. But when Samantha came back with her bear, the reporter's face fell.

'I thought you said it had lost an eye,' he said.

'He did,' said Samantha. 'But we had him mended.'

The reporter and the photographer murmured together for a moment. Then the reporter said, 'The trouble is, it doesn't make for a very good picture. If we promised to have it repaired for you, would you mind if we took out the eye again, just for the photo?'

What?! Samantha was horrified. She clutched Albert to her chest and burst into tears.

'That's lovely,' said the photographer and

flash!

flash!

flash!

went his camera, capturing Samantha in a perfect moment of misery.

The next day, while Jamie was at school, his mum went to do a bit more decorating at the toymender's. When she arrived, a van was blocking the narrow street and a bundle of cables trailed from the van into the workshop, which was packed with people and ablaze with lights. A young woman holding a clipboard sat facing Mr Patchett, who looked extremely nervous. A cameraman hunched over his camera and a sound man held out a pole with a microphone on the end of it, which hung over the toymender's head.

'Running,' said the cameraman.

The woman with the clipboard said: 'Mr Patchett, a lot of people are going to find this story very strange. What would you say to someone like that?'

'Well I quite understand how they feel. If I hadn't experienced it for myself, I might well suspect that it was just a lack of pies.'

'Cut!' said the interviewer. 'A what?'

'A pack of lies,' Jamie's mum called out, smiling as the toymender caught her eye.

'Let's try that again,' said the interviewer.

It went better the second time. 'But to anyone who still doubts it,' Mr Patchett added, 'I'd say: wait till it happens to your child. Then see whether you seal the fame.'

'Cut!' called the interviewer. 'Don't worry,' she told the toymender, 'we'll just carry on. 'Do you have children of your own?' she asked next.

'No, unfortunately not,' said the toymender. 'But of course I meet quite a lot of children through my work. Not so many as I used to, it's true, because these days –'

'Yes, quite,' the young woman cut him off. 'So what's your plan to save Christmas from disaster?'

'The trouble is, we don't know where he's going to strike,' Mr Patchett explained, while the interviewer nodded. 'So it's not really possible to have a poolproof flan.'

Everybody looked at each other.

'Keep it running,' said the interviewer. 'So is there anything each of us can actually do about it in the run-up to Christmas?' she went on.

'Certainly there is,' replied the toymender. 'For a start, it's essential that everyone keeps their eyes open. You never know where the Toybreaker might be hiding. Before you go to bed, shut all the doors and windows. If you hear or see anything suspicious, have a good look round. If necessary, search every crook and nanny.'

'Cut!' cried the interviewer.

They tried it again. And again. The third time the toymender got his words right: 'search every nook and cranny.'

The young woman gave him a thumbs-up sign.

'Oh, and if you've got one,' the toymender added, 'nail up the flatcap.'

'Cut! Cut! Cut!' The interviewer got up, walked to the door, took several very deep breaths, then came back and said, 'I think we'd better start again.'

When Liddy heard that the press had been to interview Samantha, she was disgusted.

'Why didn't they interview me?' she protested. 'I've had more things broken than anybody else! I'm the one they should be talking to!'

'But till a couple of days ago you didn't even *believe* in the Toybreaker,' Wayne reminded her.

'That's got nothing to do with it!' snapped Liddy. 'It's not fair! And who's most likely to suffer if the Toybreaker's still at it at Christmas? Me! I'm asking for a new computer, a pocket television, a portable phone - and that's just the beginning of my list. He's bound to go for me again!'

When she got home, her father was there. He'd just got back from his business trip and was looking worried and pale. Her mother looked as if she'd been crying. She had black blotches round her eyes where her make-up had run and was sniffing into a handkerchief.

'Hi, sugarplum!' said her father with a big wink.

'Daddy!' cried Liddy. 'It isn't fair! Samantha got interviewed by the newspaper and I didn't! You know all those things that got broken? Well it wasn't Jasper after all. It was the Toybreaker and I know he'll be after the mobile phone and the computer and all the other things I want for Christmas! What have you brought me from New York?'

'Woh,' said Mr Grabham-Popham as his wife started sobbing again. 'We'll talk about

Christmas later. But here's what I got you from the States.'

He handed her a little parcel. Liddy tore open presents so fast that it made you wonder why anyone bothered to wrap them up.

'Is that all?' said Liddy, looking at the little charm bracelet in her hand.

'It's real silver,' said her father, 'and you can add more charms yourself when you've saved up your pocket money.' At which point her mother let out a wail and ran out of the room in a jangle of jewellery. Most children would have been worried to see their mother in a state like this, and would have wondered what was going on. But Liddy didn't have time to wonder. She was too busy thinking about the one thing she always thought about: herself.

That evening Jamie's mum went up on the roof. It wasn't a party trick. It was just that she'd put up the second-hand television aerial herself and every time there was a strong wind, it swung round and then wouldn't pick up the signal any more. It was nearly dark as she climbed up the ladder. The tiles felt a bit slippery and there was a freezing wind. She crawled to the chimney, took hold of the icy metal pole and twisted it round.

'How about that?' she shouted down to Jamie, who was standing by the back window with one eye on the television indoors. 'No,' he called.

She tried several other positions until he shouted,

'Yes! That's it!' Now they'd be able to see the news programme that Mr Patchett was due to appear on.

Before beginning to crawl back down the roof, she paused to look out over the houses. They looked so cosy on winter's nights, with their lit-up windows and now, here and there, the twinkling lights of a Christmas tree. If only we weren't quite so hard up, she thought. If only we were a bit more of a family. Why was it that things worked so much better for some people? Was it just like the television: the signals were out there all the time and it was just a matter of knowing how to tune into them?

'Mum?' called Jamie. 'That's fine. Come on down now. Mr Patchett's arrived. Let's go and see if it's on!'

12
Face to Face

There wasn't a house for miles around - at least, not a house that contained children - where people weren't huddled in front of their T.V. sets that evening. No one could resist the fascination of seeing someone they knew or something they knew about made famous on the small screen.

The MacFaddles sat in a row on their sofa, where they had just eaten supper. The Gorps gawped from five armchairs whose every tuck and crevice had been searched five times over. Liddy lay on her bed in her room. Her parents seemed to be having a row downstairs. Mr Patchett, Jamie and his mum too sat impatiently through items about turkey farmers, a hospital closure and a pop concert, waiting for the piece about the Toybreaker.

'Christmas is usually a time when children wait to see what surprises Santa will bring,' began a voice. 'This must be it,' said Jamie's mum. 'But in at least one town this year the mood is far from festive. In Smolton a series of extraordinary events has put everyone on their guard and left every child fearing for the safety of their new toys.'

'There's Miss Clement!' exclaimed Jamie, pointing at the screen. She'd had her hair done specially. No prizes for guessing what she was wearing. She described what had happened to some of the children in her class.

The presenter then appeared, speaking while she strolled along the street near the toymender's workshop.

'The breakages remained a mystery until one person, who had witnessed the same thing over twenty years ago, shed invaluable light on it.'

They cut to a shot of Mr Patchett at his workbench.

'Oh,' said the toymender, a bit disappointed, 'I thought they might show the outside of the shop.'

'I told you it needs brightening up,' said Jamie's mum.

'What's that you're mending?' asked Jamie, peering at the picture.

'Nothing,' said Mr Patchett. 'They just told me to pretend.'

'Toymaker Isaiah Patchett,' said the voice.

'Toymender!' he said. 'Can't they read?'

'Shhh!' said Jamie. 'I want to hear.'

They listened while the presenter described the Toybreaker as an evil sprite or a hobgoblin. But what could be done to stop him, she asked. Mr Patchett came on and gave his answer about keeping doors and windows shut. They all sat waiting for the next question when suddenly the scene changed to a police station.

'Is that all?' said Jamie's mum.

'They didn't use very much of what I said,' remarked Mr Patchett.

'Shhh!' said Jamie again.

A police officer with very big ears was explaining that they were doing all they could but that they weren't really equipped to deal with this sort of thing. He gave a phone number for people to call if they had any experience that might be helpful. Then the programme switched to an item about a dangerous level crossing.

Following the piece on television and the newspaper article, the campaign against the Toybreaker gained strength. Several mice and a couple of cats got the shock of their lives when people who should have been asleep pounced on them in the middle of the night, suspecting they were the Toybreaker. Two burglars were actually caught red-handed by grown-ups wielding umbrellas and rolling-pins. No one caught the Toybreaker, though, but at least with everyone watching out for him he was having to be more careful. Or so it seemed, unless he was just saving his energies for Christmas, which was now only eight days away.

No more than two incidents had been reported since the broadcast. One was a drum belonging to Giles.

Its skin had been slashed so that at the first bang it would split in two. The neighbours were relieved when they found out, since Giles, with the cotton wool in his ears, didn't realise how much noise he made when he was drumming. Come to think of it, that cotton wool may have been why Giles didn't hear the Toybreaker creep into his room.

The other victim was Natasha. Her most prized possession was a set of Russian dolls - the ones that twist apart in the middle and fit one inside the other.

They'd been a present from her grandmother, who came from a place called the Russian Steppe - a vast, windswept plain which Natasha had always imagined as a kind of giant staircase.

She often took the dolls out of each other and lined them up, from the smallest to the biggest, to admire their painted clothes and their rosy cheeks.

The lacquered wood they were made of seemed as thin as egg-shell. But one morning the biggest one wouldn't open.

She gripped it as tight as she dared without risk of crushing it, but it wouldn't budge. She tried to twist it one way then the other. In the end the strain was too much for it. The wood of the outer doll shattered, cracking one of the dolls inside. Only the tiniest, inner doll remained undamaged. Her father examined the pieces and found a dab of glue where the two halves met - a new touch, that: to break a toy with something which you usually use to mend one!

There were only four days to go till Christmas. A handsome tree stood in Jamie's living room and his mum had brought home an old set of coloured lights she'd found in a dustbin at the office where she cleaned. She hoped that with a bit of luck she'd be able to get them working. She spent all evening fiddling around with them, testing them over and over again without any success. Then, just as Jamie was getting ready for bed, she told him to come down for the great lighting up ceremony.

'Ready?' she said, and flicked the switch. The Christmas tree lights didn't come on. But all the other lights went off.

Jamie wasn't that surprised. What was a nuisance was that even when she went to put the trip switch back on, nothing happened. She messed around for a while with the fuse box, then decided to leave it till the next morning when she could see what she was doing.

'Can you brush your teeth in the dark?' she asked.

'Yes,' said Jamie. 'I think I know where they are.'

'We'll get those lights working tomorrow, you wait and see,' she said as she kissed him good night.

Jamie climbed into bed and snuggled under the covers.

It was the middle of the night when something woke him - not so much a sound as a feeling - a feeling that someone was in the room. He propped himself up on one elbow and went to switch on the light. Then he remembered the electricity was off. It was a cloudy night and there was no moon, but by the glow of the streetlamps he could see the outlines of the things in his room. He waited for a minute, hoping to hear a movement, but there was no sound. The hair on his neck stood on end and a cold shudder spread over his shoulders and down his back.

'I know you're there,' he said.

Silence. He heard himself swallow. Could he be imagining it?

He waited. Still nothing moved. His heart was pounding.

'There's nothing here worth breaking,' he said. It didn't come out as loud as he'd intended.

'I haven't come to break anything,' said a thin, high voice. Jamie almost stopped breathing. He was right, then. The Toybreaker was in his room. He shivered.

'What do you want then?' he asked, his eyes searching the darkness.

'I want help,' said the voice.

'Help?' said Jamie. 'That's the last thing you'll get from me!'

He suddenly realised that this was his chance to trap the Toybreaker. You may remember that his bedroom door was a very tight fit. He didn't usually close it because it jammed against the frame and the carpet and was hard to get open again. If he could bang it shut now, he'd have the Toybreaker prisoner.

'I've had my eye on you,' said the voice.

'Have you?' said Jamie, hardly thinking what he was saying but just trying to keep the Toybreaker talking while he got ready to spring out of bed.

'I nearly spoke to you the other day,' the Toybreaker said, 'but then I thought–'

At that moment Jamie flung off the covers and leapt at the door, hurling his whole weight against it. It thudded shut.

'You won't catch me like that,' said the Toybreaker, his voice suddenly squeaky. 'I can still get out.'

In a panic, Jamie tried to think what other exits there might be. He couldn't think of any. The window was glued shut with paint. And thank goodness his mum had mended that hole in the ceiling!

'Do you know why I've chosen you?' the voice continued. 'It's because we're on the same side, Jamie, you and me. We understand each other.'

'Oh no we don't,' said Jamie. 'All I understand about you is that you're mean and vicious and–'

The Toybreaker interrupted him. 'Christmas is all right if you've got money, isn't it? Don't pretend you don't know what I mean. I suppose you wouldn't want the latest computer like Liddy, would you? You wouldn't want a remote control car like Matthew? So what are you going to get? A CD maybe. Oh no, sorry, I forgot: you haven't got a CD player, have you? Admit it: you're not like the others, Jamie. And that's why I've come to find you.'

There was some truth in what the Toybreaker said. But Jamie knew that he mustn't show any sign of weakness. He knew that he must fight against it.

'You won't get anything out of me,' Jamie told him.

'I've been having a lot of trouble lately, now everyone knows about me,' the Toybreaker went on. 'And who do I have to thank for that? You, Jamie, you. So now I want you to tell them that it's not true. Tell them it wasn't me who broke the castle. You know it was that cursed cat of Liddy's just trying to get me into trouble – the same one that followed me to the toymender's and chased me down into the cellar. Tell them it's all his fault. Tell them there's no such thing as the Toybreaker! Tell them that the toymender's lying!'

Jamie let him talk. As he listened, he was trying to make out where the voice was coming from. Suddenly he thought of the keyhole in his bedroom door. Perhaps that was how the Toybreaker was counting on making his escape. Was it possible that he could get through a keyhole? While Jamie prepared to block it, the Toybreaker's voice whined on.

'The approach of Christmas fills me with all sorts of new and deliciously mean ideas. There are only four days to go before the children get their gifts. But Christmas isn't the gift for me this year that it ought to be. I've had to give up all kinds of plans at the last moment because I've found someone awake or because somebody's woken up when they heard me. People who wouldn't normally have taken any notice are alert to the slightest noise. And why? Because they know about the danger! I can't count on the element of surprise any more. In one child's room I found a mouse trap in the Lego! In another house an electric racetrack had been wired up directly to the mains. If I'd so much as touched it I'd have been electrocuted! The whole business of breaking toys is becoming too dangerous.

'I mean, there's always been excitement in it – even suspense. But now there's something I don't like: fear. Because I know that if ever I'm caught, there'll be no mercy for me.'

'You're right there,' said Jamie. 'There won't be!' And he clamped his hand over the keyhole.

'Aaah!' cried the Toybreaker. 'How did you know where I meant to escape from?'

Jamie swelled with a sense of triumph. He had guessed right! 'Mum!' he called, 'Mum!'

'No, please!' squealed the Toybreaker. 'Wait! You don't understand. It's not my fault! I can't help it! Give me a chance, pleeeease!'

13
The Toybreaker's Tale

Jamie didn't want to listen to the Toybreaker's excuses. He'd done what no one else had managed to do - he'd caught him - and the sooner everyone knew it, the better. But there was a part of him too that was curious to hear what lies the coward would come up with. He didn't feel frightened at all now. In fact, to tell the truth, he felt a bit of a hero. So what did he have to lose?

'I'll listen to you on one condition,' said Jamie. 'That you stop hiding and show yourself.'

'What difference does that make?' said the Toybreaker.

'Mum!' called Jamie, though he knew it wasn't loud enough to wake her.

'No! All right!' said the Toybreaker. 'I agree to it.'

As Jamie stared into the gloom, a figure no bigger than a small monkey slipped out from behind the desk.

'Now you stay there,' Jamie told him. 'One move and I'll call my mum. Understand?'

The Toybreaker shifted uneasily in the shadows. Being seen seemed to have weakened his defences.

'How nice to have a mum to call as soon as something's wrong,' he said, with a quaver in his voice. 'I can't even remember mine. She was killed in an accident before I was two. I can remember my father - just. But when I was four he fell ill and I was sent to stay with my mother's brother.

'He was a fisherman. He lived in a little hut near the sea. I don't think he made much of a living out of it. In any case he was very poor. All he did was live and work. There was no fun in his life. He had no friends. No one spoke to him. In fact, people found him rather frightening. They said he knew black magic. There was a story that he'd once put a curse on someone who'd stolen his catch. But he was quite nice to me to start with. He taught me how to mend nets. He told me that he knew spells to turn a pickpocket into a cuttlefish, or a swindler into a squid.

He took me out in his boat when he went fishing. I wasn't a very good sailor, though. I remember lying in the bottom of his boat with the smell of fish, feeling seasick and wishing it would end and knowing it would go on rocking for hours and hours and hours.

'Then one day he told me that my father had died. It had happened weeks ago, he said, but he hadn't told me at the time. I felt wretched. I felt as if he'd lied to me. I remember sitting on a lobster pot, looking at a trapped lobster stumbling about inside. I didn't feel sorry for it. It just made me angry. I poked it with a stick. The lobster tried to grab it with its pincers. My uncle shouted at me and told me to make myself useful. I don't remember what I answered but anyway he told me that he'd be looking after me from now on and that I had to do what he said.

'From then on he stopped being kind. If I didn't want to go out fishing with him, he locked me in the hut. I had nothing to do. He wouldn't buy me any toys. He wouldn't even buy me books to look at or paper to draw on. In winter the cold wind blew through the cracks in the walls and I couldn't get warm.

But he used to come in cold and wet from a bad day's fishing and say that I had it easy, staying indoors in the dry.

'I hated him. I was so glad when I was old enough to go to school. But even then there were problems. Some of the other children made fun of me. They called me names because of the way I looked. My clothes were worn out. My trousers were too short for me. But my uncle didn't care. He said clothes were too expensive. He was glad to get me out of the way.

'I made friends at school. But when I went to their houses, I hated my uncle even more. Some of them were quite poor. But they all had toys. I told my uncle. He was furious. He said I was ungrateful. He said he fed me and gave me a roof over my head. How dare I moan about not having toys!'

All the time the Toybreaker had been speaking, Jamie had kept his eyes fixed on him. He couldn't see any detail or colour, only a dark shape against the wall. Everything told him that he should distrust this creature, yet he realised he'd been listening to the story with a kind of fascination. He felt he should give some sign that he didn't believe it, but all he could think of to say was, 'What's your name then?'

'Ralph,' came the reply, without hesitation.

'So what happened?' Jamie tried to put a

note of mockery into his voice. But as the Toybreaker went on, he had a feeling that there was something familiar about the story.

'One day I was at a friend's house, playing. He had some little tin soldiers. Every one of them was painted by hand and was different from the others. I thought they were marvellous. Before I knew it, I'd slipped one of them into my pocket. My friend didn't notice. But when I got home my uncle did. When he asked me where I'd got it from, I pretended I'd found it on the road. He didn't believe me. He said that lying was even worse than being ungrateful. He took the soldier and hurled it into the sea.

'I only stole one other thing after that: a little paintbox that I found in a cupboard at school.

It had six small tablets of colour in it. It seemed like a treasure to me - the most precious thing in the world.

green green green green
blue blue blue blue blue
yellow yellow yellow
red red red red red
black black black black
white white white white

I never dared to use it though. I hid it under my mattress.

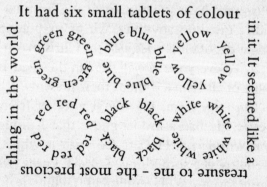

'But one day my uncle discovered it. This time he threatened to cast a spell on me.

He pointed out the
breakwaters
– those posts
that stick up in
the beach to stop
the pebbles washing
away – and he told me
that he'd turn me into one
of those if I ever stole again.

'I believed him. But I still hated him for not letting me have any toys. Even at Christmas he didn't give me anything. We never put up a single decoration – let alone a Christmas tree. I envied everyone else all the fun they had. But most of all I envied them their presents.

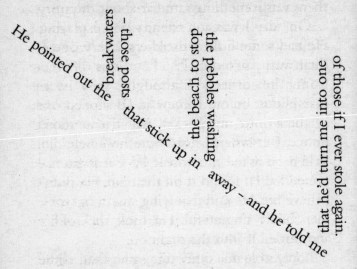

'One day I was playing at another friend's house. He had a model glider that I thought was wonderful. He left me with it while he went to get something. I don't know what came over me. I remember feeling jealous about the glider, and the next thing I knew I'd snapped off the wingflap. I quickly put it down in the grass and when he came back I pretended I'd been flying it and didn't know it was broken. He was very upset. Of course, there was a part of me that felt bad about what I'd done. But there was a bigger part that wasn't sorry at all.'

The longer Jamie listened, the surer he felt that he'd heard this story before. But he couldn't think where until the darkness itself reminded him. Of course! The first time he'd heard it, it had been in the dark too. It was the toymender who had told it, when they sat in his workshop the night they set the trap! The mean old uncle, the child with no toys: it all came back to him now, as the Toybreaker went on.

'I found myself doing the same thing again. It was a pinball machine next, belonging to another boy. I bent the pins so the balls got jammed. But this time I couldn't think of an excuse for how it had happened. The boy's parents were cross. They could see it wasn't an accident. They marched me home to my uncle and told him what I'd done. He gave me a spanking when they'd gone. But even that didn't stop me.

'I did it more sneakily after that. But eventually I was found out. When it got back to my uncle, he went berserk. I couldn't explain why I'd done it. I just knew that I wanted to have toys like theirs, and that because I couldn't, I didn't want them to enjoy them either. It didn't make sense. My uncle didn't believe me. He thought I was just a troublemaker. He said I'd ruined his reputation as an honest man. "However poor you are," he said, "you can still be honest!" "Just because you're poor," I said, "it doesn't mean you can't have fun!" He flew into a rage. "Is that your idea of fun?" he shouted. "Breaking people's toys! Very well! If that's what you want, that's what you can have!" He shook his fist at me, yelling some terrible curse in words I didn't understand. And the next thing I knew, I was like this.'

'You didn't get sent away then?' said Jamie, remembering that this was how the toymender had ended the story.

'That's what my uncle told everyone. How did you know that?' asked the Toybreaker.

'I know more about you than you think,' said Jamie. He was still enjoying the feeling of the power he had over him. One shout to his mum and he could still have him caught and handed over. But the truth was, the story he'd just heard had made Jamie feel a bit strange. He could imagine how he'd felt, with no toys at all, living with that mean uncle. Then suddenly, with a shudder, he realised how easily he had been drawn into believing it.

Even though it seemed to fit with the toymender's account, it was still possible that the whole thing was a web of lies. He decided to test the Toybreaker a little further.

'And you've been like this ever since?' he said.

'Yes. From that day on, the only thing I've wanted to do is break the toys that children care about. It's the only thing that makes me happy. I can't help it. Everyone does what makes them happy. Even people who spend their lives doing kind things for other people only do it 'cause it makes them feel good. And breaking toys is what makes me feel good.'

'Toys like the puppet whose strings you tangled and whose nose you broke at that toymaker's?' said Jamie. 'And whose foot you cracked when you came back to tangle it again?'

'How do you know all that? You weren't even alive then!' squealed the Toybreaker. He clearly didn't realise that the young boy from those days was the same Isaiah Patchett who now mended toys in Smolton.

'That was the first time you nearly got caught, wasn't it?' said Jamie. He felt a kind of heat rising inside him. 'And the last time was at the toymender's here. How did you get away that time?'

'There was a hatch in the pavement,' the Toybreaker said, 'that they used to use to deliver coal and things to the cellars. I slipped out through that.' His voice had changed. He sounded cornered, defeated, afraid.

'Lucky,' said Jamie. 'But your luck's run out now.'

'But I can't help it!' whined the Toybreaker. 'I have no choice! It was a curse!'

'If it's a curse,' said Jamie, 'there must have been some way out of it. Why didn't you try to find one? Or did you think you'd just go on doing it forever?'

'I don't know!' said the Toybreaker. 'I thought perhaps my uncle would lift it after a time. But if he meant to, he never got the chance. He went out fishing one morning when the weather was bad.

Before long a storm brewed up.

The sea turned wild.

Huge forks of lightning cracked the sky.

My uncle never came back. Bits of his boat were washed up a few days later. So I never found out if he meant to give me another chance or not.'

'Anyway,' said Jamie, fighting off the sympathy he felt welling up inside him. 'Now you're caught, so it's all over.'

'They'll kill me,' said the Toybreaker.

'Tell them your story,' said Jamie.

'They'll never believe it!' said the Toybreaker. 'They've got too much to hate me for.' Jamie could hear the fear in his voice. He peered through the darkness at the small shape, cowering against the wall. Almost against his will, he found himself believing the Toybreaker's story.

'What if you stopped breaking things?' he said. 'Maybe you'd turn back to a boy again.'

There was a silence.

'You can't undo what you've done,' said the Toybreaker.

'I've been right about other things,' Jamie added, 'haven't I? So maybe I'd be right about this too.'

Jamie could feel that the Toybreaker was thinking about it. But after a moment, 'I can't,' was all the Toybreaker said.

'Isn't it worth a try?' said Jamie.

'How could I?' asked the Toybreaker. 'At

Christmas, of all times!'

'If I keep you prisoner here,' said Jamie, 'you won't have the choice.'

'You can't keep me prisoner forever,' said the Toybreaker. 'Anyway, you'll have to go out of the room sooner or later, and then I'll be able to slip out too.'

'O.K. I'll call my mum then,' said Jamie.

'No wait,' said the Toybreaker. 'If I do what you say, how do I know it'll work?'

'You don't,' said Jamie. 'But we can hope.'

'You'd have to help me. You'd have to let me stay here. Once I'm outside, I won't be able to resist breaking something. You can't imagine what it feels like. Especially when it's someone who's really spoilt. Like that Liddy girl. The thought of all the things she'll be getting for Christmas makes me sick! I don't believe it doesn't make you sick - just a little bit - doesn't it?'

It did, but Jamie didn't want to admit it to the Toybreaker. 'That doesn't mean you have to break them,' he said.

'So I can stay here then, can I?' asked the Toybreaker.

What a strange thing to be happening, thought Jamie. At the beginning he'd been on his own, trying to turn everyone against the Toybreaker. And now that everyone was against him, here was Jamie, even more on his own, trying to help him!

Slowly, Jamie moved away from the keyhole.

14
A Christmas Surprise

What would you have done in Jamie's place? Would you have handed over the Toybreaker? Would you have let them have him? He would have made quite a show in the local museum, next to the shrunken head and the two-tailed cat.

When Jamie saw him in the light of day, he had to admit he looked pretty horrid: spindly, twitchy and mean. He reminded him of one of those painted wooden dolls that hang by their heads, whose arms and legs all leap up together when you pull a string.

'Would I have been so ready to believe him,' Jamie wondered, 'if I'd been able to see him?' But at least he was still there. And though he shrank into the corner, ashamed of his appearance when he felt Jamie's eyes on him, he made no attempt to escape.

Of course, Jamie knew he was taking a risk. He had no idea whether the curse could be lifted or not. But he reckoned that even if it couldn't, he might at least have saved Smolton from a miserable Christmas.

Already the television was reporting that there had been no new breakages that night. Everyone was on full alert. Police leave had been cancelled. Volunteers were organised to keep watch. And so that everyone could spring into action and try to block the Toybreaker's escape if he was spotted, Miss Clement had agreed to give the alarm by ringing the school bell. Especially in the quiet of the night, *that* would be heard by hundreds of households for miles around. Jamie told the Toybreaker about all these moves, to try to convince him of the danger he was in, and so help him not to change his mind.

'Are you coming down for breakfast or do you want to wait for lunch?' his mum called at around eleven o'clock. It was the first day of the Christmas holidays. She wasn't surprised that he'd slept in.

'No, I'm coming,' Jamie answered, adding quietly to the Toybreaker: 'You stay here. It's your only chance.'

'I got the tree lights working,' she told him. 'Do you want to see?'

The lights looked pretty, so many different colours twinkling eagerly amongst the branches, but Jamie found it difficult to appreciate them. He forced himself to make conversation and did a bit of washing up, but at the first opportunity he dashed back up to his room. The Toybreaker was still there.

How Jamie longed to share his secret with someone!

'Mum,' he said, coming downstairs at one point. But when she answered, he changed his mind. No one else had heard the Toybreaker's story. No one else would want to take the slightest chance. Jamie knew he'd have to carry it on his own.

'You've been in your room nearly all day,' his mum said to him at tea time. 'Why don't you come along to Mr Patchett's with me? I'm going to see how he's getting on with cleaning up his workshop.'

Jamie's mind reached for an excuse not to go, then he thought to himself, 'I'll have to leave him on his own some time. Why not now?'

When they got there, his mum peered through the shop window and had a nasty shock. The toymender was stretched out on the floor, not moving. She rushed to the door, pushed it open and hurried in.

'Isaiah!' she shouted.

'I was just relaxing,' he told her with a smile. 'What with all this tidying up, I've been doing a lot of lifting and bending. My track's being a bit bubblesome.'

He'd certainly been busy. The place looked much less cluttered and there were several boxes full of things to be thrown away. But Jamie's mind was elsewhere. Not a minute went by without his wondering whether his prisoner was still at home. When the talk turned to the Toybreaker, Jamie felt ready to explode.

'It's marvellous how everyone's come together against him,' said his mum.

'Yes,' said the toymender. 'Let's hope they'll get him this time.'

If they only knew, Jamie thought, that I've already got him!

It was late when Jamie and his mum eventually said goodnight to the toymender and left the shop.

A
thin
moon
was up
as they
walked
home.
It was all
Jamie
could
do not
to run
ahead
of his
mum.

He thought he'd burst as she stood at the door, wiggling the key in the lock, trying to get it to open. The second he was inside, he bounded upstairs and threw his weight against the bedroom door. He flicked on the light and looked around. There was no sign of the Toybreaker. A terrible panic welled up in him. He snatched aside the curtain. Nothing! Then something moved under the bed.

'Is that you?' he whispered.

'Shut the door!' hissed the Toybreaker.

'Jamie?' called his mum from downstairs. 'Is everything all right?'

'Fine,' said Jamie as he closed the door.

'Everything's fine.'

Over the next two days, Jamie gradually came to trust the strange creature who was sharing his room, sleeping curled up on the carpet. He stopped worrying that he'd escape when he wasn't there. It worried him more that his mum might come across him while he was out. But fortunately she was spending a lot of time at the toymender's, painting the shopfront and smartening up the workshop.

Meanwhile, not a single toy had been reported broken. The police and the organisers of the local watches were feeling pleased with themselves. Only Mr Patchett remained anxious.

'It seems to be working so far,' he said. 'But I just hope they keep watch. He may be lying low for the moment, but if I know anything about him, come Christmas Eve he'll set to work properly. It's only a tatter of mime now, you mark my words!'

As always, like a train in the distance, Christmas Eve seemed to take a long time coming and then - suddenly - it was there. By five o'clock it was dark. Jamie had left some bread and jam in his room for the Toybreaker to eat and had gone to the shops for his mum. As he came out of the grocer's he met Jonathan.

'Hey,' said Jonathan. 'Have you heard about Liddy?'

'No. What?' asked Jamie.

'Her dad's lost all his money. Apparently he was in America, fixing up some big deal, and it all went wrong. They're going to have to sell their house and everything! Looks like Liddy won't be getting all those things for Christmas after all!'

Jamie hurried home with the news. He couldn't wait to tell the Toybreaker. Liddy, of all people! The person he'd most envied! Their wealth had seemed such a permanent thing! And really it was just a bubble all ready to burst!

He dumped the shopping on the kitchen table and went up to his room.

'Well,' he said. 'You won't be missing much at Liddy's this Christmas!' He waited for the Toybreaker to come out from behind the curtains or the desk. 'Ralph?' he said. No answer came. The bread and jam was gone. So was the Toybreaker! A shudder ran down Jamie's spine: Christmas Eve! Mr Patchett had been right.

Without explaining to his mum, he grabbed the torch and ran out of the house.

But as soon as he was in the street, he realised that he had no idea where to start looking. The Toybreaker could have gone anywhere! Why had he trusted him? Why hadn't he just handed him over straightaway? He would have been a hero! His photo would have been in all the papers! People at school would never have teased him again! And instead he'd believed against all the odds that someone who'd been breaking toys for years and years would suddenly stop because he, Jamie, had suggested it! How stupid he felt! But perhaps it wasn't too late. Perhaps if he could find him, he'd still be able to stop him. Should he give the alarm? Yet how could he? He didn't know where he'd gone. And he could never own up that he'd had him in his own house and then let him go!

Half running and half walking, Jamie headed into the middle of town. He passed a group of carol singers under a street lamp. He passed a bright shop window full of toys. Then, just as he was wondering which direction to take, he heard the familiar ringing of his school bell. That meant the Toybreaker had been spotted! Jamie changed direction and headed for his school.

It was the Gorps who had given the alarm.

Samantha, looking out of her bedroom window in the dark, had spotted a skinny figure crossing their front garden. Now everyone on their street was out looking for him. People prowled the pavements, searched their gardens, rummaged in sheds and garages.

'There's one place nobody's looked,' remarked Mr Gorp, and pointed at the large skip that was sitting in the road.

The neighbours were having their house done up and all the stuff that had been torn out of it had been thrown into this *skip*. It was full of wet cement, used paint tins, broken planks, oily rags, bent nails, brick dust, bucketfuls of soot, soggy cardboard.

And guess who was now up to his waist in it, sifting through it all? Of course! It was Mr Gorp.

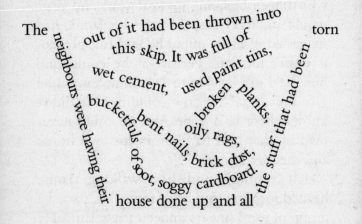

By the time he climbed out half an hour later, all black and filthy, the panic had already moved on. This time it centred on the MacFaddles' house. It was Matthew's mother herself – queen of jigsaw puzzles – who had caught sight of something suspicious lurking in the shadows. The whole family sprang into action. Mr MacFaddle had bought his wife a monster, ten thousand piece jigsaw for Christmas and was terrified that the Toybreaker would go for it. But search as they might, they found no sign of him and nothing appeared to have been disturbed.

Time was running out. In five or six hours, presents would be appearing under Christmas trees and at the foot of sleeping children's beds. At all costs the Toybreaker had to be caught before then. Everyone knew that once the clocks struck midnight on Christmas Eve, it would be too late.

Meanwhile, Jamie roamed the night-time streets, feeling miserable and as un-Christmassy as you could possibly feel.

'Ralph?' he called, whenever there was no one around to hear. He didn't know how he'd explain himself if someone stepped out of a doorway and asked what he was doing.

He pointed his torch down passageways and under bushes. Its beam picked out empty crates, a spade, a bottle, a punctured ball. A drinks can then a piece of litter jumped into colour as the ring of light settled on it. A lost glove greeted him from a railing. Then he pointed the torch up to the rooftops but it wasn't strong enough to reach.

Soon the bulb began to flicker. The batteries were fading, and Jamie's hopes with them. He knew he must get home: his mum would be worrying.

Then, as he walked past the park, a pair of

eyes suddenly glinted in the undergrowth! 'Ralph!' he called. The face turned away. The park gates were locked at night but Jamie knew a place where you could squeeze through the fence. In seconds he was crawling on all fours with a roof of holly leaves pricking his back. He scrambled out onto the damp lawn and edged his way along, hissing the Toybreaker's name and peering into the shadows under the bushes. All at once, there they were again!

'It's me!' Jamie called.

Two oval eyes blinked back at him. They stared out, full of fear.

'Come back home,' he urged. 'It's not too late. It can still work. Don't you want to be a boy again?'

The eyes began moving towards him. Then Jamie's heart sank. It wasn't the Toybreaker after all. A fat cat – wasn't it Jasper? – padded out from under the bush, paused, miaowed, then trotted away across the dark grass.

When Jamie got home, he told his mum that he'd been helping to keep watch for the Toybreaker.

'I heard the school bell,' she said. 'Any luck?' But she already knew the answer from the expression on Jamie's face.

'Never mind,' she said. 'We mustn't let it spoil our Christmas!'

Jamie kissed her goodnight and trudged up to bed.

He felt no excitement as he hung up his stocking. For the first time in days, he went to sleep with his door left open.

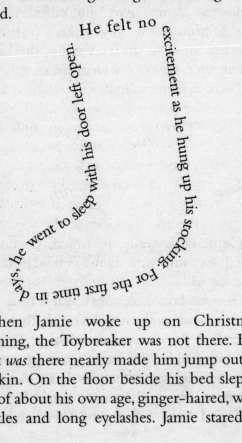

When Jamie woke up on Christmas morning, the Toybreaker was not there. But what *was* there nearly made him jump out of his skin. On the floor beside his bed slept a boy of about his own age, ginger-haired, with freckles and long eyelashes. Jamie stared at him. Who on earth was it? He had never seen him before. What was a complete stranger doing in his room? Then, as Jamie watched the boy's peaceful breathing, the incredible thought occurred to him: could this be the Toybreaker? Could it be true? Had his gamble paid off?

'Ralph?' he whispered, almost frightened to disturb him.

The boy opened his eyes and yawned. Then, seeing Jamie staring at him in disbelief, he took a glance at himself. At first he seemed almost frightened. He looked at Jamie, he looked back at himself. Sitting up, he caught sight of his reflection in the mirror that was propped against the wall. A huge grin spread across his face.

The two boys talked excitedly together for ages. When his mum came in, Jamie still hadn't looked at his stocking. She shrieked at the sight of Ralph.

'Who - what - who's this?' she stammered.

Well, you can imagine, it took some explaining! And when Mr Patchett arrived, the boys had to start explaining all over again. After he realsied that this was the very boy he had heard about all those years ago, whose story he had himself repeated to Jamie and his mum, Mr Patchett was overcome by the feeling of what a small world it was.

All four of them sat down by the Christmas tree. Its lights twinkled and its coloured balls glinted. Jamie's mum had tied little bows of red ribbon on the ends of some of the branches. Glittering strands of silver dangled from its needles. On its top perched a star that the toymender had carved from wood and painted in blue and gold.

They sat by the Christmas tree and talked and talked and talked.

'I thought it was all over,' said Jamie, 'when you disappeared last night.'

'I know,' said Ralph, 'but you see, I didn't break anything. Do you remember me saying that I couldn't undo what I'd already done? Well, I suddenly thought: there were a couple of things I could put right - things I'd taken that I could give back - if I could find them again.'

And that's exactly what he had done. Matthew MacFaddle was puzzled to find his puzzle complete. The missing piece of Noah's ark lay on the table, waiting for him to press it proudly into place. And the little key lay neatly beside Freddy Gorp's clockwork car, without his dad having to turn over a single piece of rubbish to find it. Mr Gorp felt mildly bemused, remembering all the muck that he'd rummaged through in search of it. But he didn't mind as long as Freddy was happy.

Jamie got a superb red racing bike for Christmas. It wasn't new, but Mr Patchett had overhauled and resprayed it, and it looked as good as new. His mum got a mirror in a beautiful little carved and painted frame from Mr Patchett.

All the children of Smolton had a happy Christmas, untroubled by the Toybreaker.

Only the young T.V. journalist was disappointed that nothing horrible had happened - she'd been hoping she might get onto the national news.

A 'For Sale' sign went up outside the Grabham-Popham's house and they moved away before anyone had had time to say good riddance.

As for Ralph, he went to live with Mr Patchett and joined Jamie's class at school. He was popular with the other children and became a particular favourite of Miss Clement, who was very impressed by the stories he made up about poor fishermen and wicked uncles and criminals on the run.

Having had no toys at all as a child, he was now surrounded by them at home. After school he spent hours in the workshop helping Mr Patchett. He even started learning how to make things himself. For traditional painted wooden toys were sweeping back into fashion, and with the shop completely 'refurbished' (as Jamie insisted on calling it) Mr Patchett was soon the owner of a very busy business.

'I have a confession to make,' Jamie's mum told him. 'You know when they introduced you as a toymaker on the television. It wasn't a mistake. I told them to say that.'

So Mr Patchett repainted the sign to say what it had originally said.

One evening, Jamie and his mum, Mr Patchett and Ralph met up to have a meal at the chip shop. 'I've had an idea,' said Jamie's mum. 'Why don't we all four have lunch together every Sunday?'

Mr Patchett put down his knife and fork, and smiled.

'If there's one thing I could do to make life better than it already is,' said Mr Patchett, 'that would be my worst fish.'

But everyone knew what he meant.

BY HUNTER DAVIES

It's so unfair! Flossie Teacake is always watching her older brother and sister do things that she is not allowed to do herself. But all her dreams come true when she tries on her sister Bella's fur coat, and is magically transformed from a timid ten-year-old to an extremely exciting eighteen-year-old with the world at her feet. Watch out everyone, Flossie is determined to have as much fun as possible...

Read about Flossie's many madcap adventures in these fantastic books

Flossie Teacake's Fur Coat
0 09 996710 3 £3.99

Flossie Teacake Again
0 09 996720 0 £3.99

Flossie Teacake Strikes Back
0 09 996730 8 £3.99

Flossie Teacake wins the Lottery
0 09 971151 6 £3.99

Flossie Teacake's Holiday
0 09 940372 2 £3.99

RED FOX
SCHOOL STORIES COLLECTIONS

These brilliant bumper bind-ups are packed with top-grade tales of cool characters, treacherous teachers and some seriously sinister happenings in the classroom. School has never been this exciting, so get your hands on these cool collections - they'll be an education!

COOL SCHOOL STORIES

The Worst Kids in the World and
The Worst Kids in the World Best School Year Ever
by Barbara Robinson
Wasim in the Deep End by Chris Ashley
Follow that Bus! by Pat Hutchins
0 09 926585 0 £4.99

MORE COOL SCHOOL STORIES

Runners by Susan Gates
Graphicat by Marilyn Watts
The Present Takers by Aidan Chambers
0 09 940023 5 £4.99

NEW COOL SCHOOL STORIES

The Class that Went Wild by Ruth Thomas
My School is Cool by Catherine Sides
Triv in Pursuit by Michael Coleman
The Detention by Primrose Lovett
A Devilish Dare by Nick Corrin
0 09 941121 0 £4.99

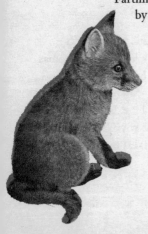